D0917720

SCUM
OF THE
EARTH

CODY GOODFELLOW

ERASERHEAD PRESS
PORTLAND, OREGON

JUL - - 2019

ERASERHEAD PRESS
PO Box 10065
Portland, OR 97296

www.eraserheadpress.com
facebook/eraserheadpress

ISBN: 978-1-62105-287-6
Copyright © 2019 by Cody Goodfellow
Cover copyright © 2019 Matthew Revert

All rights reserved. No part of this book may be reproduced or transmitted in
any form or by any means, electronic or mechanical, including photocopying,
recording, or by any information storage and retrieval system, without the
written consent of the publisher, except where permitted by law.

Printed in the USA.

JUL - - 2019

SCUM OF THE EARTH

By noontime the dock
Is swarming with men
Coming out from the ghostly freighter
They move in the shadows
Where no one can see
And they're chaining up people
And they're bringing them to me
Asking me, Kill them now, or later?
Asking me!
Kill them now, or later?
—"Pirate Jenny" by Kurt Weill & Bertolt Brecht

FOR ALICIA—
Not a song, but something to sing about… mostly.

1

Strange constellations of envious stars dimmed and faded in the pellucid night sky shimmering with fireworks above pillars of black smoke from sacrificial bonfires around the pyramids and temples of Atenopolis, Eye of the Sun, Capitol of the Fifth Kingdom.

While the city mourned the death of Tutankhaten CCXII and burned their worldly possessions under the watchful eyes of the priest-police, the smoke and lustrous explosions invoked the sleeping Sun God, signaling the pharaoh's readiness to ascend to meet Him.

Dancers gyrated in the streets, miming love acts with the departed monarch, and mourners cried out his name to the heavens, most without the incentive of the priests' electrified flails, for Tutankhaten CCXII was far from the cruelest ruler in recent memory.

Out of the public eye, many celebrated in earnest, for even the fairest pharaoh was still a prick, and the odds on the Feather of Truth outweighing his heart were running close to twenty to one; but whatever reward he earned in the afterlife, he would enjoy it far from Atenopolis, and his heir was not old enough to see over a tit, so the prospect of another royal funeral lay as far away as one could hope for.

From the apex of the newest pyramid, an onyx-faced monolithic spire to dwarf its neighbors, a solitary figure resplendent in burial wrappings of spun gold looked down on the funereal pavilion at the foot of the pyramid, where the last of the slaves and favored ones of the court were receiving their lethal injections and having their vital organs interred in canopic jars. Though a few panicked and tried to flee, the atmosphere was ominously joyous, the certainty that they were being taken up to Heaven provoking a synchronized cheer with every new death.

"Fucking idiots," muttered Tutankhaten CCXII. Flinging at the stars the sacred syringe with which he'd dispatched the priests charged with interring him, he watched it arc earthward and tumble down the flank of his tomb, and he laughed.

They came to him with their horoscopes and he'd played along; not because he cared for the will of the stars, but because he was bored. His empire ran itself like a team of oxen plowing a field from horizon to horizon. At times, he felt no freer than the lowest slaves toiling at the endless river of trinkets and gewgaws to assure their rulers' passage into the afterlife. Looking now over the grand necropolis of his kingdom and the gaudy assemblage of treasure to ransom his place in the netherworld, he hoped for more.

Even for the pharaoh, there could be no doubt about the order of heaven and earth or the dominion of Aten. He had witnessed his father's funeral ascension and seen countless demonstrations of the power of the Sun God and His sky-chariot, but he had also seen and dealt out more than enough death to have concerns about whose end the rituals were meant to serve.

Though the journey to the netherworld would be arduous and require many tithes, he had begun to wonder if most of this shit was really going to help. Did he really need a barge of solid gold? What kind of river would such a useless vessel even float on? And his slaves in the underworld would not be much help, unless death by lethal injection made them a lot more competent than they were, when alive.

The two hundred and twelfth living image of Aten wanted something no gold could buy on this world. He wanted answers, and if the god whose living image he embodied struck him down for his impudence, then he would go to judgment knowing he had only hoped to grasp the feather of truth, and add to its weight.

Tutankhaten CCXII looked up at the stars and recited the words the priest would have intoned, had the pharaoh meekly submitted to destiny. As if waiting only for the invitation, a star belled out into a fiery lotus directly overhead, plummeting out of the firmament with such roaring brilliance that the fireworks were muted as the pale imitations they were.

Tutankhaten CCXII clapped his hands and shuffled giddily to his sarcophagus atop a dais in the middle of his hoard. Yet again, the world had obligingly shown its belly, leaving the pharaoh to wonder if maybe God had only ridden roughshod over the destinies of men because no one had thought to take a firm enough hand with Him.

The sky-chariot arrived and floated above the pyramid with a sonic boom that silenced the city's rituals, deafening those too foolhardy to plug their ears with wax, blinding those rash enough to look up.

Even when the corona of heat discharge had dissipated, its form was too blazingly bright to be contained by the mortal eye. The ray of coruscating light that lanced out from its belly to envelop the pyramid was brighter still, so that only the priests with their tinted visors could look directly into it, and still they could barely make out the outlines of the tomb hoard of Tutankhaten CCXII, his golden barge and his provisions and mortal remains and organ jars of seven hundred slaves, concubines, advisors and sundry randos who couldn't bribe their way out of a crooked lottery, as they were lifted off the pyramid and floated up towards the floating sky-chariot, to disappear into its radiance.

Then the sky-chariot itself vanished with a thunderclap, and a hush ensued as the rulers of the empire awaited the pharaoh's judgment in the netherworld, and a hushed cheer as the rest of it reclaimed what they could of their belongings from the bonfires, broke out the dagga and the beer and celebrated another rich guy being dead.

The belly of the sky-chariot was nothing like Tutankhaten CCXII expected. When he emerged from his sarcophagus, the gods did not bow and make obeisance or demand he produce his heart—which he stood ready to produce, having combed the empire for the most virtuous and faithful citizen to donate one in his place. Instead, they merely shrugged at each other and shook their heads, which were as ugly as any jackals, though decidedly human in aspect.

"Fuck me," one of them said into a dull gray piece of jewelry on his wrist. He had Kushite features, but his skin was a deep metallic indigo, with weird plugs and spigots embedded in the dome of his oddly-shaped skull. "Fucking cargo's still alive…"

"Easy to fix," said the other, a brawny, yellow-haired barbarian he was alarmed to recognize as a woman.

Though he could not understand the gods' strange language, the jewelry repeated their words in his native tongue. Tutankhaten fell to his knees and began to declare his lineage all the way back to the transgressor Tutankhaten, who forsook his name and the true god Aten to become Tutankhamen I, forcing the Sun God to deliver those who truly believed to a new kingdom on a new world.

"Shut up, cargo," growled the hulking, pale woman. She drew a weird tool from a wide leather belt fortified with pouches and sheaths. When he raised his ceremonial crook and flail, she fidgeted with a dial on the tool's pommel and it turned into a wickedly curved scimitar of blue fire.

"Don't cut him up out here, you dolt," the blue Kushite said. "Put him back in his asparagus."

"Wiglaf is dolt?" she laughed and swung at the ugly one's head with her fiery sword. "Is called *sarcophagus*, lutefisk-for-brains…"

Even from agents of the Sun God, Tutankhaten CCXII could brook no more disrespect. In the most imperious voice he could muster, he demanded to be judged and conducted to the netherworld to meet his ancestors, but then he saw the looming apparition behind his tormentors.

"O Almighty Aten!" he cried out, bowing low his kohl-painted brow to the deck of the sky-chariot. "I am your own true descendent, by two hundred twelve generations of true inbreeding."

"Oi!" the Kushite barked at the one true god. "Magico, you twat, stop freaking out the cargo, and give us a hit off that spliff."

The wizened gray face, inscrutable black eyes, proud cranial bulge—all bespoke the spirit and image of the first true pharaoh, and of the drivers of the sky-chariots that bore them to the new Egypt. But his apparel was the same form-fitting, ugly nylon and Perspex pressure suit as the others, and he wore a preposterous black top hat festooned with ribbons, bones, medallions, talismans and sundry other memorabilia. He seemed none too concerned with the plight of his true descendent as he partook of the insidious weed the slaves of Atenopolis smoked whenever they thought they could get away with it, sucked it in with his lipless mouth, and blew out a perfect smoke ring that whirled and formed a staring eye of Horus, before passing it to the Kushite.

"Behold your divine likeness in my own features! I demand your judgment…"

"Told cargo shut up," the barbarian said, and ran him through. He watched with cold horror as the wide, curved fire-blade plunged through his breastplate of hammered platinum and lapis lazuli, through the layers of gold and into his breastbone, through his still-beating heart. Transfixed, it skipped a beat, but then resumed thudding against his ribs as if he wasn't impaled, but he still found he couldn't move. The crook and flail dropped from his nerveless fingers.

"Wiglaf, my own dear favorite crewmate," the blue one asked after a brief coughing fit, "has it ever occurred to you, in light of recent events, that this knob might be worth more... you know... alive?"

"Does Wiglaf come round when Skink work his job," Wiglaf demanded, "and slap dicks out of mouth?" Steering the paralyzed pharaoh by the grip of her blade, the barbarian maneuvered Tutankhaten CCXII back to his sarcophagus and deposited him therein before withdrawing her eerie sword.

He found himself still paralyzed, but he could hear and comprehend all too clearly. "Relax, old son," said the Kushite. "You'll get your judgment in the netherworld soon enough. Bad news is, everything you ever believed is a load of shit. The truth is a lot worse, but good news is, you'll probably not have to bother with it."

He proceeded to rummage through the pharaoh's burial-wrappings, pulling out several carved charms of topaz, moonstone and turquoise secreted amongst the fragrant gold bandages.

"You see, your highness, your world is only one of many far-flung shitballs all over the universe where Earth refugees have been dumped and forgotten by little green geezers no more divine than yourselves. Because honest space piracy is hard and geezers get deaded doing it, canny freebooters like ourselves take advantage of your isolation and ignorance to profit handsomely off the brisk trade in human-made..."

"Shit on me," he mumbled as he produced a golden scarab beetle inset with fire opals, clutching a dungball that was a flawless diamond the size of a walnut. "That'd make a sweet pinky ring." Plucking out and chucking the diamond, he stuck his finger through the clasp and admired it.

To Tutankhaten's utter horror, the creature he'd mistaken for his ancestor the god of the sun came over and joined in ransacking his living yet lifeless body. "Fuck off and get your own, you bogarting gray cunt, you... Anyway...

"See, most advanced civilizations can mock up all the diamonds and gold and whatever easier than taking a shit, so the most prized goods are those worked by hand, representing not just craft and mastery, but also a sizable span of a life."

Brandishing the scarab ring, he added, "Quality workmanship, yeah? Bet some geezer studied his whole life for the privilege of smithing and honing and polishing this little item, for which effort your people had him killed, so he could never make one for anyone else. This alone ought to get you into Heaven... if *you* made it..."

"Wiglaf only wanted to kill him," Wiglaf said. "This is *mean*."

"Go somewhere else."

"Skink want live cargo," Wiglaf said, "Skink must ask Captain..."

Skink shook his ugly head hard enough that Tutankhaten could hear fluid sloshing in it. "Nothing doing. Whoever asks the Captain has to *tell* the Captain, and lowly as I am, I'm not the one with that fateful duty."

"Tell the Captain what?"

"The other news," Skink replied, making a show of replacing Tutankhaten's violated burial wrappings.

"What other news?"

"See?" Skink smiled. "That magical innocence's why you get the shit duty. Now help me with this."

The barbarian came over and the three of them lifted the solid gold lid of Tutankhaten CCXII's sarcophagus, then set it in place. Even so, he still heard the deplorable looter rapping on the hammered gold likeness of his face on the lid and shouting, "Enjoy your mystical journey, your highness."

Just as the voices faded away, Tutankhaten heard Skink tell Wiglaf, "Truth to tell, I'd rather be him than you, right now... He don't gotta get between the Captain and her 'shore leave...'"

2

Shaky with post-coital bliss, Poly reclined on sweat-sodden pillows and ran her hand through her tousled auburn curls, as her fingers changed to claws, hair to iridescent feathers. Her heaving breaths settled into a slow, shallow rhythm as her lung capacity expanded, her breasts flattening and redistributing mass to her arms, which became wings.

"How about this one?" she asked, trying to keep need out of her voice even as it rose to a piercing avian trill.

Naked but for thigh-high black suede boots and gloves and a carbon-steel patch over her ruined left eye, the slim, supine body sprawling across the rest of the bed stirred so that the ruthless right eye appraised her new shape from beneath the fall of gleaming chrome hair hiding her face. "Dismissed."

"Do you want some water?"

"Hell no," said the other. "Fish fuck in it."

"Are you tired?" Why was she trying so hard?

"No," said the Captain, rolling over and coming up on her knees, then crouching, muscles tensed. "I'm *bored.*"

"Oh…" Poly felt her own muscles screaming with fatigue, twitching as they tried to divine the cloudy form in her partner's guarded mind. They'd played for hours, a progressive three-ring sideshow circus of anatomical oddities and death-defying sex acts. Played and laughed together and for a while, the Captain seemed almost enraptured by her, fascinated by her potential, but every time she'd come and collapsed laughing and Poly thought at last she'd won the game, her captain would roll over and drink, snort or smoke something, then demand that she do another one.

A wilder one, a weirder one, a more beautiful and dangerous one.

Poly had run taken a watch and a half to run through her entire repertoire, but she could not exhaust the Captain. She perched on the pillows, quivering, uncertain what to do next, but fatally certain that she would choose wrong, and all of this would be over.

"How can you be bored?" She knew she should cop an attitude, but wasn't feeling all that cocky. Still, her raw red clitoris ballooned out from under its hood into a formidable erection. When this failed to elicit any interest, she added cartilaginous ridges, augmenting herself until her cock looked like a hammerhead shark. At least now she was only trying to get a laugh, but not even that worked. "I can become anything you can imagine…"

"That's your problem," groaned Captain Callista Chrome. "You can't surprise me, can you? I want something I *can't* imagine."

She sighed and let her body go cephalopod soft, her mind go blank until she felt the Captain's psychic presence as an adamantine unrest, giving no hint how to unlock it. She was exhausted and yet she struggled to recall the pictures on the bulkhead in the Captain's private water closet. Maybe that would do it. She conjured up her memory of the most dangerous, beautiful one in the collage of dogeared photographs…

Why was she trying so hard? What was she so afraid of?

This creature had saved her from certain death when her true nature was exposed on Heliogabalus, the pleasure planet of the Coal Sack Nebula, but had no reason not to drop her off somewhere even worse, the moment Poly ceased to please her.

Was it her nature to submit so desperately to any captor? No, she had hid and run many times, rather than give herself up as she had to this vicious cutthroat, and her heart still beat faster as she regarded the captain's face.

The first time she saw that face in the casino on Heliogabalus, betting on blind-man's death-sports, she had recognized her from holo-vids and rumors, but never dreamed of approaching her, when her Wangrovian pimp had popped off about trusting the perceptions of a one-eyed pilot.

"True," Callista Chrome had said, "having only one eye does impair one's depth perception." Producing a slim crystal holdout pistol from the bodice of her corset, she dialed down the intensity after a moment's glance across the tabletop arena with the miniaturized blind men stalking each other with scythes and vibro-daggers. Then she pointed the pistol at the man and shot him in the face.

Security had surrounded her but were consulting their health benefits plans in their HUD's when she holstered her pistol and apologized to the mouthy pimp, who suffered only second-degree burns with enormous blisters over the entirety of his face from the precisely calculated laser.

Poly had laughed with everyone else, but it was upon her that solitary, inescapable eye rested upon, and Poly had found herself inescapably drawn by its gravity.

A *cruel* face, if you had only one word to describe it. Beautiful, if two, but the competition would be stiff, because *confident* and *calculating* would lie in wait to usurp the berth. But it was hard to look away from, and without even realizing she was doing it, Poly organically arrived at a more tantalizing stratagem than mimicking one of the Captain's old lovers.

Her intact right eye drooped and shut, the patch over

the left a black impassive shadow under the tumble of unruly reflective bangs. The whetstone tension in her haughty cheekbones relaxed. She might have been feigning sleep when Poly completed her transformation and crept across the bed towards Callista, who lay prone on the sheets until Poly straddled her with knees pinning her arms to the bed, before springing her ambush.

"How about this—" she asked. Callista flipped her easily onto her shoulder blades with such vehemence that the breath mashed out of her lungs, and was holding that selfsame laser pistol over her blinking violet eye.

"Is this some kind of joke?" Callista's face contorted in fury as she looked down on Poly and saw herself, perfectly mimicked, down to the sheen of sweat and more intimate fluids gleaming on her skin.

"I'm sorry. I… I tried to read your… feelings…"

"Then you read wrong, because I *don't* feel." Leveling the pistol, she shifted her weight until her groin mashed against its twin. Biting her lip, pinching Poly's nipples and raking her belly, she scissored her doppelganger harshly until they both came, the Captain with a frustrated sigh, Poly with shameful abandon.

"Change," Callista said, reminding her of the pistol, now dialed to maximum range. "Don't look at me with that fucking face."

"I'm so sorry," Poly said, "I only wanted to—"

"What? To shock me? Dominate me? Make me fall in *love* with you?" Pushing her cunt one last time into Poly's so she moaned even as the Warpie's features rippled and reknit into the doe-eyed jailbait shape she'd worn in the casino. But this only made Callista roll her eye. "Are you even a natural female? Did you come onto me as a femme just to make me trust you?"

"Well… don't you trust me? What could I possibly try to…?"

Callista laughed harshly. "You want me to trust you? Show me your true form."

Poly shivered. The words splashed her livid skin like hot oil.

She could endure anything, mimic any shape she'd ever traded proteins with, but to bare her true form to a Stone Face—as her people thought of species incapable of mimicry—was beyond mere nudity, a transgression of mating instincts far beyond the imperative of any mere cultural custom.

The hostility, the scalding malice behind the question, made her hackles rise. And before she could look at herself to find out what hackles were, they emerged from her skin as thorns of barbed bone. Protective instinct that didn't distinguish between literal and rhetorical threats had her rearing up on the bed, dewclaw spurs shredding the pillows, down feathers everywhere, but at last she got a rise out of Callista Chrome.

"You want to kill me," Callista said. Reaching up onto the headboard, she grabbed a bulb of amyl nitrate and burst it under her nose. Touching herself as she gasped with the rush, she said, "Stop digging, you've struck gold."

This time, Poly played the aggressor, and the Captain earnestly fought her for it. She sustained grievous flesh wounds as she grappled the Warpie, but by guile and willingness to sacrifice, she turned the tables even as Poly's attack became genuinely deadly, and soon pinned her with her legs, straddling her gnarled, metamorphic face with her dripping cunt.

Snarling, Poly strained to tame her raging form, to reach her captain's sex and kiss it tenderly and beg forgiveness, but she could tell that the Captain had already lost interest. "Just when you start to get interesting," she said, "you get boring again."

"Maybe you don't know what people are for, if you think we're just here to entertain you…"

The Captain put a gloved finger to her lips. "Shhhh… don't turn this rape into a marriage." The Captain rolled over, winding herself up in the sheets, and at the edge of the bed, curled up and reached for her smoking kit. "You want to make yourself useful, be a love and run to the replicator and fetch me some premium Queen of Pain blunts. And some salve for these gashes." She touched a finger to one, and when it squeezed a gasp out of her, she dug deeper, biting her lip but getting something out of the simple pain that Poly hadn't been able to give her in nearly eleven hours of continuous, polymorphous fuckery.

Fighting back tears, Poly grabbed her tunic, stepped into it and laced up the back as she ran for the exit hatch to the communal living module within the belly of the *Barracuda*.

Her raging angst over the disastrous affair was sideswiped by the other anxieties she'd kept at bay when the Captain had invited Poly to her quarters.

For one, the *Barracuda* itself, which was actually a gigantic organic, spaceborn starfish. When she'd asked why the ship wasn't simply called the *Starfish*, Skink had looked at her like the biggest idiot he'd ever clumsily hit on. "Well, that'd be pretty obvious, innit? If we called it *Starfish*, then everywhere we'd go, people would know it was us. It's like camouflage, innit? 'Sides, the Captain likes that godawful song…"

For one unused to interstellar travel at all, the Barracuda was a particularly unsettling experience. Skink told her the starfish were terrestrial marine life that had not only survived the death of their gas-torus homeworld, they swiftly evolved into starfaring behemoths several miles in diameter, and spread across the galaxy in a glacial diaspora accelerated by hot-rodding internal parasites like themselves stoking fusion reactions in their labyrinthine stomachs.

When Callista Chrome's crew hijacked the immature starfish that became the *Barracuda*, they replaced its vestigial nerve node with a navigational computer that was also a "quantum uncertainty drive," which allowed to them to drop into spacetime literally anywhere, for less than the cost of a decent eighth at any reputable pot dispensary.

Whatever any of that meant.

What she did understand was that the cramped plasteel modules were foreign bodies grown or surgically inserted into an unspeakably beautiful living creature, which probably harbored very strong negative feelings about its exploitation.

She shuddered whenever she passed through raw, organic corridors between the modules, avoided touching the glistening pink walls of the coelomic cavities or the rippling dynamos of its unbelievably vast gonads. She gave a sigh of relief when the hatch sphinctered shut behind her, although now she found herself confronting the spearpoint of her doubts and dread over her new companions.

The wardroom module was nestled in the center of the starfish, between the pyloric and cardiac stomachs, with the bridge directly overhead, a ladder ascending up a tube in the unfortunate mega-echinoderm's anus. Chairs, beanbags, hammocks, blowup-dolls, hookahs, sticky VR rigs and a couple battered pinball machines were distributed in what looked less like the dayroom of a starship than a cut-rate opium den. A lopsided bug walk rhythm burbled out of the blown-out intercom speakers.

The crew of the *Barracuda* sat or sprawled in their seats around a dinner table strewn with wrappers and debris from countless nutritional and pharmacological catastrophes, but the object of their current absorption seemed to be an enormous gray-green slug, which writhed in its slime.

"Wait your turn, Skink."

"But it *is* my turn, Wiggy. Can I be blamed if your short-term memory is a fucking sieve? Pity a big girl like you, can't handle her slug…"

Skink leaned in to lick the bubbling head of the slug, which withdrew its perturbed eyestalks just in time to avoid the poxy humanoid's greedy gray tongue. He froze with said tongue dangling out his mouth when he noticed Poly cringing in the corner of the common room. "Ah, look what the cat kicked out! Someone looks to be ready for their initiation into the club."

"Be nice," Wiglaf said, scooting over in her chair and patting the warm, sweat-dimpled seat beside her. "Come, sit. Be not sad. Enjoy slug."

Poly looked round the table, at the blonde giantess from

the planet Warworld III; at the skeevy colloidal silver-tinted man from Planet Grime with sockets and shunts in his skull and chest, and a straw snaking out of the base of his skull into the corner of his mouth that allowed him to sip his own cerebrospinal fluid; at the living mummy of dully glittering gray flesh, empty black eyes, only the sharklike grin assuring her of the very worst intentions betraying anything like humanity at all; at the sleek, muscular black dog-thing sitting upright and smoking a cigarette.

She moved towards the latter of this motley crew, but the dog growled and laid back her ears so her long, narrow skull looked like a claw-hammer with fangs.

A welter of brutally vivid images pummeled her brain. *You dead bloated and green/Dog buries snout in your anus/Dog rips out and feasts on festering intestines/Happy Dog!*

"Shut up, Lilith," Wiglaf said.

Skink said, "Bitch's just jealous of anyone who smells like her mistress. She'll ignore you once you've had a shower."

"Is she an Earth dog, from Earth?"

"Not quite," Skink said. "Sick geezers spliced her with human DNA and juiced up her temporal lobes for telepathic exchange, so while she ain't got the sense the gods gave a buttplug, she makes her feelings known clear enough."

Poly gathered herself. If she was on trial here, let her defend herself. "I didn't ask to join your crew. I only need a ride home…"

"No one's inviting you to join our crew, darling," Skink said, slouching out of his chair and crossing the room to the replicator unit bulging like a breast out of the bulkhead.

As he fiddled with the replicator's settings, he added, "You've already joined a far less select group, but with a proud record of achievement, nonetheless."

He took something shiny out of the tray and presented it to her with a bow.

It was a belt buckle of organic resin, coated in brilliant chrome, depicting a cowgirl getting bucked off a one-eyed bronco.

The legend above the bas-relief image said, I STAYED ON FOR 1.5 DAYS! On the back, it said, Poly MORPHOS, and the current date.

"Is not fair," Wiglaf said. "Captain picked up girl a week ago…"

"We were run out of Heliogabalus with the Imperium on our fetlocks, Wiggy. She doesn't get credit for the time her nibs was too busy to seal the deal."

"Captain was excited about her."

"It doesn't say I KEPT THE CAPTAIN WAITING, on the buckle, does it? I'm just saying, there has to be a standard, otherwise, geezers will second-guess the belt…"

"Is no good to cut buckle now. You don't know it's even over…"

"You see the look in her eye as well as I do, and you know what it means. We all do, don't we?"

Skink, Wiglaf and el Magico all hoisted their pressure suits to reveal their own tarnished belt buckles. Lilith snarled and snapped at Skink when he turned her around to show the belt buckle on her collar.

Poly's face fell. To think of how she felt, of what she'd dreamt of asking the Captain, so wrapped up in her own illusion was she that the feelings she felt were so overwhelming, so magical, they must also be mutual…

"Oh dear," Skink said, "you thought it was something special, didn't you?"

"You know nothing, none of you! What we shared, you can't even imagine…"

"Oh, but we can. We've all got our talents… We all took the tumble."

"It wasn't like that! I felt it, we both did! We were in love!" She flung the belt buckle at them. Lilith easily caught it and started chewing on it, but Skink wrested it away from her.

"You don't want it, we'll just add it to the wall." He pointed a penlight at a shadowy corner of the module, where the light splattered off a wall of tiny, gaudy headstones, each representing a hook-up, a conquest, an affair, a desertion.

All of them laughed at her. She felt her hackles begin to rise.

"Don't get excited," Wiglaf said, her hand on her sword. "Better to find new way to be useful."

"What do you do? How could I help?"

"Smuggle. Steal, deal drugs, raid. No kidnap, though. Too messy."

Skink said, "I'm sure we could all come up with a lot of ways you could be useful…"

Wiglaf hit him. "Shut! Poor girl-thing still in love."

"Fuck love," Skink said. "It's the most primitive, potentially damaging way to try to get high. It's the equivalent of making fire by rubbing two fucking sticks of wood together."

El Magico took out a snuffbox made from a pink oyster shell and sprinkled some tinsel-glitter-dust on a saltshaker beside the badly abused slug, then flicked a bit of it at Skink, who immediately lost track of the conversation for the pounding of Tchaikovsky's love theme from *Romeo & Juliet* in his ears.

"If I'm not useful, what'll happen to me?"

"We'll sell you."

"You can't just sell another intelligent living being, it's unethical."

Wiglaf retuned the translator on her wrist gauntlet and held it up to the slug on the table. The slug's writhing emerged as a faint, high, plaintive voice. *"Would you like to hear a poem I composed?"*

Wiglaf took up the saltshaker and dashed a bit of it on the slug's back.

"Unhand her, you mendacious gunt!" Skink lunged across the table and slapped and clawed at Wiglaf, trying to reclaim the saltshaker.

The slug twisted on itself in a soup of violently expelled bodily fluids. Its keening scream of mortal agony emerged from the translator as a hauntingly beautiful form of music, until el Magico popped the whole thing in his mouth.

"Taste it," Wiglaf said, holding out a dab of the firefly-glowing slime. "Girl-thing never heard music as lovely as this tastes. You'll get over love."

Poly pouted and covered her mouth.

Skink was still trying to climb over her to get to the saltshaker. "Don't listen to them, love! You run through my veins. Don't let us be apart another instant…"

Skink followed the saltshaker when Wiglaf tossed it, stuffed it down the front of his trousers and scrambled, giggling insanely, out of the wardroom.

"How long will it last?" Wiglaf asked el Magico.

With an elaborate shrug, he replied that nobody knows in affairs of the heart, but Skink was a very shallow man who always courted his own unhappiness, and he pointed out that the poxy human had also abducted the pepper mill.

"So," Wiglaf said, "no more distractions. Who will tell the Captain?"

"Tell the Captain what?" Poly asked, immediately feeling foolish when all eyes turned on her.

"You want to be useful," Wiglaf said, "there you go."

"Yes," said a husky voice from just over her shoulder, "which one of you is going to tell me the Bad, Bad News?"

Poly shook her head. "I don't know what they're talking about, I don't know anything—"

"That much, I believe." Callista Chrome pushed Poly into a beanbag hammock and strode over to glower at her crew. She wore a gorgeous silver feathered kimono that snapped and breathed green fire that licked down her lean, powerful limbs as she restlessly paced the common module. Poly wondered if she was really in love with this strutting, mean, mad person, or if she had been drugged like the poxy man had been drugged into running away with the saltshaker. If there was any difference, in the end.

"Which of you was going to tell me what happened to Earth?"

Wiglaf, Lilith and Magico all looked at each other, practicing their most sincerely clueless, *Oh shit, what happened to Earth?* faces, while Poly earnestly trotted out her kneejerk, *What the shit is Earth?* face.

Wiglaf finally said, "You always hated that place anyway…"

Callista kicked over a pinball machine. "How can I fucking count on you people with my life, when I can't trust you to give me bad fucking news?"

"How'd you find out?"

"That's the best part," she said, suddenly eerily calm, which made at least one of those seated at the table wet their chair. "Because none of you ass-clowns could sack up and tell me, I had to hear it from the narc dreadnought racing up our assholes, right now."

"The what?"

"Oh yeah." With a flourish and a snap of her fingers, the Captain brought up a conglomerate aft view, looking out the eyespots at the tip of each arm and down the trails of exhaust from their tube-foot thrusters at an R-class Starblood dreadnought cruiser, fully capable of dismantling all but the most strongly godlike planetary defenses, fifteen sectors off their six o'clock and closing at an alarming rate and working to shut down their wireless portal, because nobody had sounded the alarm.

"*That's* how you deliver bad news," Callista Chrome said, as she climbed the rectal ladder into the bridge of her pirate ship.

3

So yes, the Earth was destroyed.

And while this might come as a grave surprise to anyone who didn't realize they were contained within a derivative space opera, the only real surprise to most of the sentient universe was that such a drastic step was not taken long, long before.

Though they remained woefully ignorant of other intelligent life beyond their own world, humankind had long been a source of much controversy throughout the galaxy. Most regarded them as a hazardous and corruptive invasive species despite the many, many useful products derived from conscientious farming of their bodies and brains, while the nameless aggregate of benevolent alien artificial intelligences dedicated to enforcing a modicum of civilization through the known universe classified humankind, with remarkable pragmatism, as a Schedule 1 Controlled Substance whose debatable self-awareness was a trivial consideration next to the appalling toxicity brought about by extended contact with them and their works.

Their dreaded enforcers, the Intergalactic Narcotic Enforcement Force—known colloquially as the narcs or, for reasons that shall presently be made plain, the yeasties—were the ones who had burned Earth, but the rush to exploit them had made it inevitable.

And Margie, that bitch.

"Try to think of something relaxing from your childhood," Margie the anesthesiologist in the orbital departure salon told Noreen Costello, "and then take a deep breath." Nobody in the fateful chain of events set into motion that ordinary morning could be blamed for what would transpire as a result of the voyage of *ISS Sally Ride* to the fledgling Bifrost colony on Mars; but many historians looking for a culprit in the ultimate destruction of the Earth point to that well-meaning busybody anesthesiologist, and her disastrous fucking advice.

In spite of the space program's best efforts—soothing music and aromas, hypnogoggles, foot massages and teledildonic therapy—the experience of being sedated and frozen for the three-year voyage was still entirely too much like dying by lethal injection in a 20th century prison.

Even the most seasoned space travelers tensed up at the last moment with spontaneous anxiety about the journey, which was as far from Earth as civilians could travel, and not entirely foolproof. More than one interplanetary ship simply vanished without a trace, or turned into savage abattoirs when the food synthesizer broke down or "What's New Pussycat?" got stuck on repeat on the intercom.

Bifrost was little more than a mining town with a preternatural abundance of orphans and unclaimed bastards, and in dire need of resourceful teachers such as Noreen Costello, who abandoned her floating condo in sunken Coral Gables and auctioned her U.S. citizenship shares to buy the ticket.

Travel sites chronically preached that the last thoughts tend to fix and resonate in the frozen brain, so a jittery preflight experience could leave a nervous passenger an icy tuning fork of distress for the duration, which left the newly arrived tourist or emigrant fatigued, with increased susceptibility to mutated spaceborne viruses, venereal diseases from improperly vetted outworld prostitutes, and sundry other hazards of the new frontier.

Some pray as they go under. Some visualize a beloved pet or a calm day at the beach. Noreen was nervous enough to bolt or wet herself right before freezing, which would fuck up their launch window, or force them to eat a delay voucher, which was coming out of Margie's ass. Maybe she genuinely felt concern for Noreen, who by all accounts, looked like somebody's dusty spinster aunt, and had an annoying tendency to make everyone around her feel eight years old.

Noreen found her calming image as she inhaled the gas, and never thought or dreamed another dream again. But she, at least as much as Margie, doomed every last inhabitant of the planet Earth with her stupid memory.

As inevitable as the foreshadowing that foreshadowed it, in the midst of their journey, at a point in interstellar space distinguished today only by a plaque that keeps getting stolen and a truly miserable souvenir shop, *ISS Sally Ride* was waylaid by a space pirate corsair which effortlessly defeated the humans' laughable defenses, then proceeded to depressurize the habitation modules, defenestrating the live crew, before boarding.

The pirates were Xrulshi—huge, viciously stupid flightless carrion birds from parts unknown who had somehow acquired near-lightspeed travel without inventing the written word. A savage race known only by the unsettling noise they made in the depths of their wattled throats as they kill you, the Xrulshi keep their own counsel.

Ergo, no record persists of what they thought of, or how they disposed of the cargo—seeds and embryos for a laundry list of useful Earth flora and fauna, a small fleet of orbital dropships, machinery and materials for the colony, as well as the four hundred passengers themselves—but what happened next was like that hypothetical moment when early homo sapiens first tossed a pig in a fire and discovered bacon.

Nor can we say what possessed the bored Xrulshi cargo thrower, an exceptionally twitchy specimen of that species, to do what he did. Perhaps the same impetuous curiosity of the bacon-discoverer above, or perhaps that unknowing pawn of destiny that fucked a green monkey to bring his species AIDS. It is universally recognized that the brightest sparks of momentary genius are often kindled among imbeciles who truly hate their jobs.

Charged with cataloguing and storing the frozen humans, the cargo-thrower happened to notice the output port in the medical monitor panels was a primitive analogue of the interface on his recreational holo rig, on which he liked to watch other giant flightless birds being plucked and beheaded.

(Thus, by such weird convergences does God demonstrate that, far from playing dice with the universe, She often can't be bothered to flip a fucking coin.)

With a few slight modifications, an input jack was adapted to fit the port and the intrepid emu-creature plugged into a randomly selected human passenger.

Instantly, the wearying world of the corsair's cargo hold whisked away on a silver wind that chilled the Xrulshi cargo thrower's poikilothermic blood.

For a moment, he was an immature human girl in thick but close-fitting thermal false plumage, gliding across the glassy water ice of the millpond behind a Lutheran church in Braintree, Massachusetts.

She had been practicing all autumn at the YMCA ice rink, but her instructor and her mother shouting at her from the penalty box made her so nervous, she'd fallen again and again; but without anyone shouting at her to focus or watch her form, she gracefully turned her blades so she was flying into a spiral and launched herself into the air, auguring the cold with her spinning form, throwing wide her arms so she became a blur, and just this once, stuck the landing, gracefully flying backwards across the ice like a creature born to it.

The memory lasted only as long as it took eight-year-old Noreen Costello to land her first double axel, replayed over and over again as a flickering synaptic misfire in the flash-frozen human brain; but the experience opened a floodgate of sensory impressions like the aftertaste and half-imagined notes of a fine wine.

And then something magical happened.

The effect on the cargo thrower was immediate and powerful. Found drooling dreamily beside Noreen Costello's cryogenic pod, he was subjected to a serious stumping—half his tail removed, with no means to grow it back until returning to whatever unlucky, fucked place the Xrulshi hail from—but word spread round the ship and soon, the captain was about to jettison all the cryogenic pods because the crew's jacking into them was interfering with even the minimal duties involved in near-lightspeed interstellar travel.

Hardly any of the frozen passengers yielded any coherent memories, only impressions of deep anxiety and fear, and none of those that did were quite so precious as Noreen's. Fighting broke out over use of her port, bringing down the captain's wrath, until a brighter light under his command suggested that anything so irresistible to these bloody-minded dimwits might be worth more than the live humans themselves, which were valued more for their leather, than their labor, on the current intergalactic market.

All this we know because the Xrulshi corsair turned up at a waypoint station near Rigel with Noreen and proceeded to pimp her as an entertainment. The line of savage alien bounty hunters and raider scum waiting to skate the little millpond stretched out of the tavern they'd hired out and swiftly attracted the notice of spaceport security, who broke up the party and blasted poor Noreen out an airlock, but not before someone made copies.

Although only a few aloof interstellar empires hold the secret of faster-than-light travel, quantum information transfer via wireless rendered those copies across the stars within hours. Somehow, without modification for wildly varying nervous systems, the dream of the double-axel edged out hard and digital drugs as well as online gambling, interactive snuff and virtual sex. More sophisticated experiential rigs essentially allowed users to freebase Noreen's cherished childhood memory in such obliterating clarity that one's own memories seemed like unwelcome brown background noise, better off forgotten— the soreness of her chafed, bruised thighs and behind, the cold nipping at her fingers and nose, the anticipation of hot cocoa with melted miniature marshmallows beside a roaring fire, added to the rich complexity of the little girl's anxiety, defiance, determination and exultation in the course of the successful figure skating trick.

Its cumulative effects were so potent that intelligent lifeforms all over the universe began to turn up dead of dehydration or other fatal self-neglect with Noreen's memory playing on loop in their brains.

Though it was hardly the first time humans cropped up at the center of a controlled substance controversy, the viral outbreak of the Ice Skating Memeory was like crack cocaine showing up in white suburbia. Pirates, drug-runners and miscellaneous entrepreneurial scumbags began to violate the long-standing interdiction zone around Earth's solar system, smashing and grabbing every frozen human brain they could find looking for the next ice skating dream. Where only the lowest of lifeforms had resorted to consuming human brain products like dopamine, endorphins or oxytocin, memory jacking had no such stigma, and played in the most exclusive salons of the galactic core, though the new trade was hardly any more humane than the old. Hapless human guinea pigs were thawed, force-fed hormones and hyper-compressed stimuli and then refrozen, in hopes of recapturing that special magic.

The interdiction zone around Earth had long been patrolled by Intergalactic Narcotic Enforcement Force dreadnoughts, but enterprising smugglers still managed to penetrate it with sad regularity, and human "stash colonies" seeded all over the Milky Way galaxy still provided a ready supply of humans for both licit and illicit commercial purposes.

The real source of the problem was not humanity itself, progressive drug reformers complained, but the uniquely awful nature of the human brain itself, which, aside from producing a host of remarkable psychoactive chemicals, had the almost unique capacity, in all the universe, to lie to itself. It was this ability to fantasize, to imagine things as other than they are as a therapeutic refuge from the cruel indifference of the objective world, and thus to fabricate self-sustaining bubble-realities, that led more highly evolved cultures to decry the interstellar pollution sown throughout the cosmos by decades of irresponsible Earth television broadcasting, and to demand some permanent solution before every race in the universe became equally obsessed with creating art and fiction and new religions instead of focusing on provably worthwhile activities like applied evolution of slave species and the Genocide Lottery.

So it came to pass, that when the narcs descended on Earth and scorched its surface to bubbling molten slag, its irradiated atmosphere combusted and blown away on the solar winds, its people exterminated to the last lead-lined box containing the last perfect egg and sperm specimens, most of the universe breathed a sigh of relief and turned its attention to more complex and satisfying problems, like learning how to ice skate.

4

"Attention unregistered ship… The human homeworld of Earth has been purified by mandated military action as a threat to public health. Our intelligence indicates probable humans and/or human-related contraband onboard your vessel. You will cease all activities immediately and prepare to receive downcast inspection agents of the Intergalactic Narcotic Enforcement Force, or be destroyed. Our intelligence indicates a high statistical unlikelihood to comply, so prepare to be destroyed… This transmission may be monitored or recorded to insure that you are destroyed…"

"You are my one and only," Skink murmured to his beloved saltshaker. "Don't listen to their lies. To them, you're only an inanimate object to be emptied and refilled, they can't stand to see us happy, they want to tear us apart… I've never, never ever used any other condiment, you're the taste of my tears…"

"Put your girlfriend away," said the Captain, "or I'll take her away. And cut off that fucking message."

The crew sat at their consoles on the cramped bridge of the

Barracuda. Captain Chrome lounged in her swiveling egg chair with a cigarette in a headset, leaving her hands free to work the controls of the starfish, now flailing its way across interstellar space at two-thirds light-speed, and still losing ground to the Enforcement Force dreadnought.

"Wireless report, Skink!" Callista kicked Skink in the back with her stiletto heel so his head bounced off his monitor.

Something rebooted inside him and he shouted, "No downcast incursions on my board, milady. Boffins seem to want to run us down old-school."

Callista quirked her lips in dismay. The yeasties didn't generally go in for running space battles. Having jammed the universal wireless network, they were quite capable of downcasting a virus into a ship to shut it down, turn its atmosphere to lethal chlorine gas or implement specs for a nanobot wasp nest or other gruesome means of enforcing their inscrutable will.

As *Barracuda's* second mate, Wiglaf wore many hats, but in a pursuit situation, her primary duty lay in keeping such underhanded tactics from knocking them sideways until they could deploy the warp drive. She had such hopes the first time she wore her new war-helm, and Skink had ruined it for her.

"You know," Skink had said, "real Vikings didn't wear horns on their fucking helmets, Wiggy."

"Not so," she protested, pointing to the reference photos she'd fed into the replicator: mighty Norse warriors, gods and goddesses, all with big fucking horns on their helmets, but he laughed at her.

"Popular misconception, old heifer, foisted on you by costume designers for an especially dreadful form of cultural torture perpetrated on Old Earth, called *opera*. You don't look a proper Viking, you just look like a cow."

Wiglaf was so discouraged, she broke the horns off and sulked. Skink said it'd be nice to finally have fresh milk, so she tried to jam them up his ass.

Now she wore the helmet with the broken stumps like the crown of a cold, ugly country.

"Deploy countermeasures," Callista said to Wiglaf, who eagerly mashed buttons stimulating the starfish's gonads to expel clouds of nanobot factories in their wake. By the time the dreadnought passed through them, they would be a tornado of deadly whirling projectiles that would slice through their repulsor shields and bore into the hulls. The chance of anything organic onboard that might be distressed by a loss of atmospheric pressure was practically nil, but any distress incurred on the enemy might give them a razor-thin edge, and let them escape.

Wiglaf was just glad for the opportunity to kill something. "Countermeasures away," she said. "How about missiles? Wiglaf has many missiles…"

"That'll do for now."

"What about gonads again?"

"That'll do, for fuck's sake."

Curled at the Captain's feet, Lilith yawned and stretched her lanky limbs with disturbingly humanoid digits at the end of her massive paws, clawing at the stained shag carpeting on the deck. Abruptly, her ears perked up and she turned to look behind the Captain, a warning growl deep in her throat.

Poly the Warpie waif peered in at them from the aft hatchway. "The replicator in the wardroom is going crazy," she said. "What do I do?"

"We don't bring problems onto my bridge," Callista grated.

"Go turn it off, girl," Wiglaf said.

"I tried that already! It's spraying out silicon goo…"

"Get the fuck off my bridge!" Callista hit a button on the arm of her chair and a steaming bulb of espresso popped out. She caught it in her teeth and crushed it, hissing at the heat. Then, into her headset, "Magico, why is our warp drive still sober?"

As the ship's medical officer, el Magico, belowdecks in the

starfish's mouth, was responsible for the warp drive, for reasons that shall soon become obvious.

El Magico's impassive face appeared on an inset screen on the monitor tracking their encroaching, unstoppable demise. His shrug said, *The warp drive is watching a really great nature documentary, and says you should all check it out…*

At first glance, el Magico was what any student of twentieth century Earth culture, or just a peruser of the free bin outside any used bookshop, would recognize as a Gray, the emaciated saucermen lifted to mythic status by unreliable rural witnesses gripped by bad meth and pre-millennial angst.

With his bulbous skull, tapered face and elongated, boneless-seeming limbs, he presented a hideous apparition that could've answered a lot of nagging questions and put some conspiracy theories to rest, and he had no end of trippy anecdotes if you shared a spliff or a few peyote buttons with him, but every time the story was different. Whether he was a scientist from the future, an angel, an exiled prisoner from a parallel dimension or just an android body aliens from unguessably distant worlds used to terrorize primitive civilizations for kicks, he turned on with a Peruvian shaman and dropped out of the abduction trade, joined a rogue CIA hit squad, and was the secret puppet-master behind the People's Temple and Heaven's Gate cult suicides, depending on what drug he was on, and whether he was trying to bang you.

What was not open to debate was that he was the galaxy's foremost authority on controlled substances and holistic healing, both of which came in useful on a ship where the crew got bored and hurt each other a lot.

But something was wrong belowdecks. The warp drive wasn't responding and Poly wouldn't shut up about the fucking replicator. *So help me*, thought Callista, *if the wardroom is full of fucking belt buckles again—*

The dreadnought, still gaining on them, had fired no weapons, though they could easily disable or disintegrate the

Barracuda at will, but they weren't even firing defensive layers to cut a path through the nanobot cloud. Was it just their horrible luck to have blundered into the fuckers who wiped out the Earth, or was this absurd overkill actually being deployed to run them down?

"Open a wireless channel, Skink... *Skink!*"

Wiglaf batted the saltshaker out of his hand. It fell on the console and cracked. Skink held the broken saltshaker high, dumping its granules onto his tongue. "Turn my blood to gravy, my love! I don't want to live without you!"

Poly wailed, "Somebody better get down here..."

"Goddamnit, Wiglaf, see to the mimic." The giantess reluctantly pushed back her console and went below.

"Lilith," Callista called, pointing at Skink. "Sic 'im."

The dog-creature didn't have to be told twice. Pouncing on the first mate, Lilith snapped his wrist in her jaws and swallowed the broken saltshaker. He cried and she licked his face, but then he remembered he still had the peppermill, and seemed to gather his composure. "I'm sorry, Captain..." Strapping his fractured wrist into a brace from a handy dispenser, he said, "I've been most unprofessional."

"We all fuck up. That's what we do. But what do we do next?"

"We unfuck it, ma'am."

"We've been compromised, and your boards don't even show any incursion."

"The narcs is some sneaky geezers, milady, but we're topped up on their line of evil. Even with the saltshaker up my arse, I could've kept them at length."

"So maybe it's not the narcs," she said.

"But wait..." He pointed at the screen. "What's all that, then?"

Just at that moment, Wiglaf's board lit up as the pursuing dreadnought passed into their nanobot corona and nothing happened at all.

"Aren't they supposed to light up and rip open and blow

up, leaving us a clear path to run free?"

"Something like that, your majesty," Skink mumbled.

"Fucking cheating cunts! What about that wireless channel?"

"It, um… It's been open for a while, ma'am."

"Your insults have been duly recorded and added to your crimes," a colorless, uninflected voice oiled their ears. A brace of missiles and a salvo of lasers were fired at them. At this distance, the lasers could have cut them up instantly, but they seemed to be conserving energy by targeting manually, using the lasers to pin them down for the missiles creeping up on their tail.

"Cut the shit," the Captain barked. "We know you're not the narcs."

"Then what are you running from?" The colorless voice came not from the bridge speakers, but from the port behind the Captain's chair. From whence Wiglaf and Poly had gone, and not returned.

"Captain," Wiglaf called out, "please to come see this, please."

"Kinda busy right now. What is it?" Callista asked, but a dreadful sinking feeling told her she already had a bad idea what it was. But why couldn't people just tell you what the fucking problem was?

"What is it, just tell me?"

"Just to come see."

"You know how much I hate that! Just tell me!"

"Then when you see, will be redundant…"

The first missiles popped the collision alarms. Callista ripped the *Barracuda* out of its previous flight path and corkscrewed between the missiles, which obligingly homed in on and destroyed each other.

Looking from Lilith to Skink, she ordered Lilith to take her chair, and went back to the ladder.

Suddenly, the ship lurched like it had a bad cramp. The bridge went black except for the glow of her cigarette. Callista's feet spun out from under her as her forward momentum flung her into a freefall minefield of debris. Porno disks, coffee cups, Styrofoam cartons, sex toys, cigarette butts and spaghetti tangles of disconnected patch cables.

Instantly, they'd lost propulsion, power, life support and grabbity, which could only mean one possibility, Callista thought with rising panic. Someone decapitated their computer. Well, two possibilities, if their computer had once again forgotten that it was a computer, and was getting buggy ideas it was still human.

Catching the ladder with one arm, she whipped around and scuttled down, making a torpedo of her slim body so she shot into the wardroom module ready to kick the shit out of whoever or whatever had invaded her ship.

"What the blue fuck," she demanded.

Wiglaf and Poly were ensnared in hentai tentacles of hardening silicon and at their nexus, an exoskeletal proto-humanoid form with an extravagant, glossy pincers at the terminus of its armored abdomen. It looked like a monstrous cross between an earwig and a silverfish, like something you'd step on without hesitation, if it scurried out from under your dishwasher, but it stood a head taller than her and opened its arms in anticipation of their imminent collision.

Wiglaf cried out, "Don't touch it, Captain, it's—"

"I know what it is," Callista said, but she was already crashing into it. At the last instant, she triggered her static shield, enveloping her body in a crackling electrical aura. She still bore the brunt of the impact, but the ersatz organism she hit shorted out with a violent implosion. Callista passed through it and smashed into the bulkhead in a smear of inert silicon paste, rebounded and came at Wiglaf.

"How many more are there?" she demanded.

"Two, Captain. I'm sorry, I tried to stop them…"

"They're mine," she said, and kicked off the bulkhead in the direction of the engine room, leaving Wiglaf moaning to be cut free.

There was no time. You had so much of it to waste, you'd do anything to get through it, and then, when you needed it, where the fuck was it?

She put on a bold face for her crew, but if this was what it looked like, they were truly fucked. And by *they*, she meant to include every human settlement, gulag, refugee camp and backwater empire they'd ever visited, which accounted for just about every human being left in the universe.

Spinning, she caught a thick cable bundle and pulled herself down a narrow interstitial corridor, noticing something streaking along the wall beside her. She reversed course and pointed her laser pistol, nearly burned a hole in Poly before she realized the mimic had freed herself by turning into some sort of arboreal meta-primate.

Poly bared her teeth and plunged ahead of the Captain. Stupid minx was going to get herself fried, which might solve two problems, Callista thought wryly, but that wasn't fair. It wasn't the alien shapeshifter's fault that no matter what form she took, she still had her head up her ass. Trying to impress someone who was dead inside wasn't love, it was just delusion.

Where was she? Oh yes, downcast invaders on her ship, fucking up everything she owned.

She popped into the engine room to find, as advertised, two more silicon earwigs. One was freefall grappling with Poly, who gouged wads of silicon out of the thorax of her opponent with four razor-clawed arms, but to no discernible effect.

The other one was methodically disconnecting the ship's computer from the web of cables and flukeworm sucker-mouths, and plugging it into itself.

The moment it accessed the computer, it would know everywhere they'd ever been and how the quantum uncertainty drive worked, and it could go there instantly and harvest them like any other contraband cash crop.

She blasted the thing's head off, but of course, it did no good. Clicking and humming heedlessly to itself, the earwig decoupled the last plug on the breadbox-sized cylinder and spun out a compatible dongle to insert into it, when Callista shut her eye and fired again.

The laser blast speared the computer's housing, causing an explosion of plasma and gray slush, It also pierced the earwig, which inclined its neck-stump sorrowfully as it regarded the wrecked computer, and then dissolved into so much floating soap scum.

Poly disentangled herself from the husk of her disabled earwig and floated as close as she dared to the Captain. "Well done, Captain."

But Callista was wracked with sudden, violent tears, and shook her off violently when she put an arm around her.

"We stopped them, didn't we?" Poly asked.

Callista didn't answer. All around them, the starfish trembled and thrashed in the void, suddenly cut loose of the parasitic organisms enslaving it, but then Poly, Callista, the two dead earwigs and all the random junk around them fell to the deck as something like acceleration took them in its grip.

Falling to her knees beside the blasted computer, Callista put a hand on its surface, swiped up some of the gray matter and dabbed her lips with it. "I'm so sorry, baby... So fucking sorry..."

Poly put a hand on her shoulder, recoiled as the muscles tensed beneath her fingers. "It's OK, Captain. We'll get a new computer..."

Callista whirled on her, face a mask of agony. "You don't know anything! This was my..."

Then everything went white—

And then black.

5

As a species whose native tongue was purely chemical, their name was a rancid taste in the back of the throat, like ammonia, curdled milk and more ammonia. For the sake of their non-pheromone speaking customers, they called themselves the Mercantile. None of them seemed to have individual names. Aside from a myriad of disposable drones, those who sold their products to the public were simply called Merchants, while those charged with expanding and protecting territories, punishing competitors and thwarting regulators were known as Interlocutors.

Their roles were best seen as analogous to the difference between worker and warrior ant castes. But the Mercantile apparently had crystal brains with no chemical activity whatsoever, but only electrical impulses. So its mind was nimble, pragmatic and utterly ruthless in pursuit of the only pleasure it seemed capable of experiencing, the acquisition of profit and dominance of its customers. Thus, though no living organism in the known universe could be said to be more fundamentally different from human beings, they made incredibly effective drug dealers.

Looking up at the Interlocutor looming over her now, Callista Chrome had to remind herself she was not smaller than an insect.

"Ah, you're awake. Wonderful! Perfect! Now, we can begin our conversation." Its voice was fruity, mellifluous and not at all slurred for having no lips, tongue or teeth. She figured a speech synthesizer was installed in one of its palps.

She was naked except for her eyepatch, and felt as if she'd been scoured with brushes and industrial solvents. Probably looking for bugs, nanobots or other contraband. The Mercantile were nothing if not thorough.

She lay on a soft, unpleasantly warm bench in a featureless cell of the same resinous silver-gray material as the Interlocutor itself. Actually, there was a hole like a garbage-disposal, presumably for solid waste excretions, but it was set into the wall a few inches below the ceiling, and the grabbity on this ship was turned up half-again as much as she liked.

"You mean torture."

"No no no! Of course not! I am not an interrogator and this is not a torture chamber, bless your dysfunctional sentience. This is not to be an ordeal, but a warm and free exchange of ideas."

"Here's a free idea. I want my clothes back."

"Ah, but it's vital to get off on an equitable footing. I am naked, you are naked. Nothing to hide. Just two naked lifeforms, casually enjoying their nakedness. A perfect jumping–off point. Why don't you like being naked?"

"Maybe I'm just jealous of your kickass exoskeleton," Callista said.

If the Interlocutor detected her sarcasm, it chose to ignore it for the sake of decorum. "I should be the uncomfortable one, if we're being honest. In addition to your odious mental functions, your reproductive organs are no picnic for me to look at, either. The very concept of exchanging and conjugating genetic material is utterly repulsive to our person…"

Preening forelimbs scraped at its chitinous shell with a

sound like dry ice on steel. Crystal-whiskered palps protruding from its otherwise featureless face combed each other lasciviously, and she suddenly tasted moldy tortillas and semen. The Interlocutor lacked the generative organs to consummate whatever awful proposition it was silently floating, but clearly fancied itself an attractive partner. Callista chose to ignore it for the sake of keeping her lunch.

"Fine, fuck the clothes," she said, stretching, giving the earwig a good eyeful. "Can I at least have a fucking cigarette?"

"I'm afraid we can't tolerate open combustion on our vessel, but if you require nicotine…" A palp with a syringe attached to it darted out and pricked her neck. She cringed and swatted at it, but her reflexes were far too slow. Her heart beat faster, her nerves sang. She felt a calming hand pressing her down into the bench. She swatted at that, too, a couple times, even though it wasn't there.

"So…" the Interlocutor folded itself until it crouched level with her eye. "Since I am your host, I shall start. I have nothing to hide, and I hope that once we've shared with each other, we might leave this cell not as mistrustful antagonists, but as mutual beneficiaries of an enlightened understanding."

"You hijacked us."

"You're pirates. Was it not an appropriate method to reach out to pirates? Anyway, no one was seriously harmed…"

Callista twitched, feinting the kind of heated lashing out attack the Interlocutor might've hoped to provoke, but it gave no response. Even if she could somehow tear the thing's head off, they would only send in another with the same questions, the same supercilious, rancid flirting…

"I am sorry about your computer, but if we can come to an understanding, I'd be happy to replace it…"

She scowled.

"Oh, I realize it had what you call sentimental value, which effectively cubes the practical value of any product, but you have only yourself to blame. You should have cooperated. You'll feel even worse, when you realize the rewards we always hoped to offer you, for your cooperation."

"You want to corner the market on humans."

"You require protecting. Your home planet has been destroyed by the puritanical Yeast."

"*You* destroyed my home, by making it a target."

"Oh, there's that human imagination we prize so highly! Your fascinating little ship and your charming crew are unharmed—"

"And you still haven't said shit that means shit to me."

"I'm trying, but you're not making it easy. Do you require more nicotine to comprehend what I'm saying?"

She vehemently shook her head.

"Very well. You see, economic progress operates with the same punctuated equilibrium as any other evolutionary process. For centuries, humans have proven useful for their slave labor and unique brain chemistry, but in combating the memory holo epidemic, the INEF has actually tipped the market towards direct cranial stimulation. The civilized lifeform wants an implant to directly affect their brains. Only the lowest gutter-races still use drugs, no offense."

"So, we're still a marketable commodity. You must be happier for us than we are. Keep squeezing us, you'll be sorry."

"There it is again! That wonderful imagination! Your utterly irreproducible way of lying to yourselves, your capacity for fantasy, is precisely what makes you such a temptation, that the Earth had to go.

"You see, the Costello Ice Skating memeory was a game-changer, but it was only the beginning of a qualitative change in the human question. It transcended the interspecies barriers that made your cultural pollution warfare mostly harmless…"

"You mean our movies, our music…"

"Yes, the pride you take in your imaginary bubble-universes, those adorable totems of self-delusion you humans call art, never gets old.

"Imagination. Every other species that did not outgrow the

compulsion to delude itself died in its terrestrial cradle long before reaching the stars."

"We didn't exactly reach them, though. We were dragged."

"That, in my personal estimation, is why you humans cling to such a dangerous cognitive aberration. When you are always the center of your own myth-cycle, it frees one from petty obligations like gratitude."

"You'll get a lot of things out of me before you get a thank-you for what you fuckers did to me and my kind."

The Interlocutor didn't respond at once, the vague bulges of its eyes unfocused. Was it communing with the nest, or just staring at her tits? Would tits even mean anything to a neuter hatched from an egg and fed electrified nectar from a communal nurse-drone?

"This conversation has deviated from its true intent," the earwig said. "Allow me to correct it.

"Our Investigator caste closely examined the Ice Skating fad, and realized that if one wafer-thin slice of holographic memory was enough to make drugs obsolete, then offering a completely interactive open-world immersion in a living human imagination would set the market on fire..."

Callista drew in a cold breath redolent of the Interlocutor's proposal. It was sourer than its awful idea of sex. "You're talking about Boltzmann brains."

The Interlocutor nodded eagerly. "I've heard them called that, yes! A human brain, cut off from all outside stimuli, generates an interior world composed of memory and dream. Indeed, your foremost philosophers and authors used to indulge themselves with the notion that all exterior phenomena were suspect, as one could not prove one was not a brain in a fishtank.

"So this should seem like heaven, to many of you."

"Having your brain be a playground for rich alien assholes? Yeah, it's exactly what we always prayed for."

"To live eternally in your own imaginations, to be kings of infinite space inside a nutshell, or however it goes... It would not only corner the drug market, but the entertainment field, and religion might even come back in style, if everyone had the opportunity to be a god in their own universe…"

"In our brains."

"Yes. Given your past career as a freebooting exploiter of human colonies, we thought you'd jump at the opportunity."

Cocking her hips provocatively, she said, "You have no idea what I'd jump at."

"But we've seen enough holotapes posted by your former crewmates to make an educated guess."

"So you want my opinion?"

"It would be ever so edifying, yes…"

"It's garbage. You're garbage. And you should've just killed all of us honestly—"

The Interlocutor's drug-palp shot out and poked her in the neck again. "That wasn't nicotine. I hope now, you'll find it easier to behave.

"Perhaps because or in spite of our other perfections as a race, we do admittedly lack a capacity for innovation. We wish we could take credit for the idea, but as noted, we did get it from your solipsistic philosophers and comic books… and from you."

Her face reddened as if slapped. "From me?"

"Absolutely. You showed us it was practicable. Or rather, your human computer, is that the proper term for what he was?"

She shook her head. "I'm not talking about this with you…"

"Someone dear to you completely committed to memory a working tesseract. No small feat for such a primitive, anomalous brain, but at no small cost, yes? No minor sacrifice, that. Did he give up his body willingly, or did his brain simply fail to interface with it, once it had gained the secrets of the universe?"

Callista shivered, but she wasn't going to cry in front of this inorganic cockroach.

"No," the Interlocutor went on, "he must have had no choice. Perhaps he did it to save you, have you thought of that? Naturally, you have. But by connecting him to that marvelous exoterrestrial lifeform, you gave him the body he always craved, and the means to reach the stars. You used each other, and he seemed no worse wear. Your ship's medic tells us he also powered your warp drive, such as it is…"

"Magico wouldn't tell you anything…"

"Oh, he never stops, but almost none of it is worth knowing. He brags that he has only to induce a state of intoxication such that your poor navigator's brain forgets where it, and thus, the ship drops out of consensus reality, to appear instantly at any other point in his mental model of the universe. It's quite ingenious, really, in a wildly irresponsible way…"

"No one wanted to sell us a proper warp drive."

"Did you ever worry that he might forget that there are only one of each of you? With one drug addict for a warp drive and another one giving him directions, there might be more than a few evil mirror-universe Callista Chromes roaming the spaceways, as we speak."

"Pretty sure *I'm* the evil mirror-universe version of me," Callista said. Running her fingers through her hair, shorn to peach fuzz on her left side, hanging down to her elbow on her right, making her breasts dance. Yes, he was definitely watching them. Suddenly, it was a he.

"So… you wanted my ship's computer to tell you where the remaining human colonies are…"

"You must admit, it was the simplest way to get what we need."

"Oh, certainly. And since that's off the table, you're willing to make me a partner, if I just lead you to the last living humans in the universe…"

"You do understand!"

"So you can cut their brains out, can them and let aliens rape their dreams for eternity. Does that make sense?"

"I wouldn't put it quite that way, but you have a knack for vivid overstatement. Perhaps you could parley that into a spokesmodel position, when we're ready to go to market."

Lowering her arms, letting a deep breath roll her breasts irresistibly, she said, "Why don't you give me another shot of whatever that was, big boy."

The Interlocutor leaned forward, drug-palp quivering, needles dripping with anticipation. "More nicotine?"

"Surprise me," she purred. He complied, pricking her three times in rapid succession so she flushed and giggled and let him think she was about to swoon.

Fucking idiot.

"And here when I woke up and saw you, you know what I thought?"

"What did you think?"

"I thought how sad it was, that you lacked the organs to pleasure a female."

The Interlocutor shuddered. Instinct might have saved it, but the sheer perversity of the idea of coupling with this female outlaw of an interdicted race seemed to be turning the creature on.

"I am well aware of your legendary charms, Captain Chrome," it said, drawing itself up, but then lunging in to poke her again, it couldn't help itself. "Also your duplicity, your promiscuity, and your infamous tolerance for narcotics. If you do decide to seriously consider our offer..."

"Oh, I've got an answer for you," Callista said, extending her middle finger. "Do you need a universal translator to figure it out?"

The Interlocutor shook its head, more in sadness than anger. "I'll return when you're more amenable to productive dialogue."

Callista bit down on the tip of her middle finger and pulled. The digit snapped free of her hand, drawing out a two-foot length of glowing monofilial wire, out of which she made a lasso.

The earwig threw out three limbs to block the attack and two more to hit an alarm claxon, but Callista was no longer playing slow. The wire encircled it twice before it could do either, and without doing anything, it fell to the floor in five distinct chunks of cauterized meat.

Callista retracted her rigid digit and picked over the Interlocutor's remains until she found a foreleg, then keyed the lock release with it.

6

As conveniently as any lazy writer could hope for, the cell opened on a detention ward with several other communicating cells. She could see Skink pacing, Wiglaf doing pushups, Magico rolling a joint out of leaves of his own shed skin, some asshole in an Egyptian pharaoh's outfit flagellating himself with a solid gold flail, Lilith chasing her tail, and Poly recumbent in a shape like a Rhyloquin dire-cat, serenely grooming her extravagant quills and blood-red pelt.

Callista paused at the last cell, fascinated. This girl could be anything, would do anything for her. She seemed like more than the full package. Why the fuck couldn't she make her happy?

Sighing, she hit each of the locks and rallied her crew. They came staggering out, looking her over with varying degrees of lust, envy and amusement.

"OK, you losers… My eye is up here… We've been jugged, but if none of you talked, we'll get out of this not much worse than we walked in…"

Nobody was buying that.

"If we really were facing the narcs, we'd all be dead. As it is, we've just got one Mercantile ship to deal with…"

"I'd rather take on the yeasties," Skink called out.

"And we have the advantage…"

"How's that, exactly?"

"We're inside them, moron."

"Seems to me, that's exactly how they fucked us."

"Exactly."

Skink poked at something that looked a bit like a computer console. "I can't even with this shit. It fucking stinks, and I dunno how to stink back at it."

"So we'll play to our strengths."

"The violence?" Wiglaf asked hopefully.

"Yes dear," Callista said, touching the giantess's cheek. "The violence." Then she turned and shouted, "And a full bonus share on our current cargo to whoever finds my clothes."

"I can be your clothes…" Poly started to say, the suggestion bringing the biggest laugh of the shift.

"Thank you, but no. Who the fuck is King Tut, here?"

"He's the current cargo, ma'am," Skink said, really fast. He'd cross-wired his adrenalin feed so he was rocking on his toes, playing with his electro-whip in a dangerously reckless fashion.

"Gimme your clothes."

Tutankhaten CCXII was outraged, but could offer little real resistance when they removed his loincloth and tunic, leaving him swaddled in several dozen yards of spun gold, like a fucking peasant.

Wiglaf snapped off the longest of the Interlocutor's legs and whittled the claw into a spearpoint. Skink ripped some cable out of the wall, rigged it to a weird, sparky organ in its abdomen that worked like a battery. El Magico ripped off its pincers, then shoved an arm up its asshole and painted the gleaming blue silicon shit on his face like war-paint, which seemed to get him really fucking high, but then, nearly everything did.

Poly tried on a variety of fierce shapes until Callista came over and whispered in her ear.

Poly smiled. It was prettier than any of her shapes.

And scarier.

Walking around inside the Interlocutor's ship was not unlike rooting around inside its body. It was made of the same shit, impossible to figure out, and new horrible smells were around every corner.

Corridors turned and twisted, climbed and dropped in blistering disdain for handicapped access, terminating in cavernous spaces with hundreds of octagonal doors reaching up to the ceiling, and no signage.

The first drones they came to approached them with their plasma rifles extended. Callista nudged Poly forward, but she balked.

She looked exactly like the Interlocutor Callista butchered, but couldn't get the odors right. So they'd had to stick the speech synthesizer in amongst her mandibles.

"I beg your pardon, but these honorable friends have satisfied our needs, and require escort to their ship. Would you be so kind as to assist them?"

The odor translation was an unpleasant outgassing from breathing holes in her groin, armpits, thorax and legs. It smelled like burnt hair and bleach, then magnolias and a Summer's Eve douche, then vanilla and scorched maple syrup.

Their reply smelled like the third week of a garbage strike.

"Wiglaf, we're fucked.."

"Aye?"

"On the right. When I say—"

The drones looked from Poly to the others, standing about ten feet back. They aimed their rifles.

"Now."

With no other ranged weapons, she had no choice but to

flip up her eyepatch. Squeezing her facial muscles to connect the circuit, she looked right into the eyes of the drone on the left, and blinked.

The discharge caused her ears to pop and made a low *znnfff* sound almost immediately enveloped by the explosive rearrangement of the drone's squishy innards by the violent application of radical convection.

Callista hated to use the skullgun. Aside from the headaches, it drew upon her body heat and bioelectricity and magnified it a couple million times, leaving her shaky and depressed.

Thankfully, she wouldn't have to use it twice. Her target was boiling from the inside out, vomiting up strings of pearly organs when Lilith pounced on it and gratuitously ripped its head off. The one on the right fell flat on its abdomen and sat there with Wiglaf's spear transfixing its thorax.

"Well done, Wiggy," Skink said. "You'll earn those horns back yet."

Poly said, "I'm sorry, I tried…"

"You fucked up. It's fine. We'll fix it."

Poly hung her earwig head in shame. "They were telling me everything I asked. They seemed to trust me… until you people attacked them." A horrible turpentine stench emitted from all her breathing orifices. "I know where the ship is."

Callista brightened at this. "Where?"

Waving arms to waft her stink under their noses, she said, "I just told you."

Wiglaf and Callista picked up the plasma rifles, and they all ran for it.

Finally, they came to a cargo hold with an open port looking out on the stars. A few Merchant drones spooked when they saw them, but Wiglaf burned them down before anyone could raise the alarm.

Suspended overhead in a tractor beam web was the Barracuda, and beyond the static pressure barrier lay freedom.

Both might as well be a million miles away.

"What do you mean, the tractor beam shutoff is somewhere else in the ship?"

"Just that… I'm sorry, it's not my fault. I didn't design it, and I don't know why it's on a hard-to-reach console on a ledge overlooking a two-thousand foot fall into a fusion reactor intake… It's just tradition."

Skink said, "Magico and I can go shut it off, Captain. He said he's felt a strange disturbance, as if…"

"Fuck both of you." Callista strode to the controller's board, which featured a big, inviting joystick. "Well, the shutoff isn't here, but the grappler is."

Taking hold of the joystick, Callista tugged and squeezed, watching with devilish delight as the *Barracuda*, a mile across, bobbed and dipped in the air over her head like the claw in a skill-crane game.

The tractor beam web was a magnetic field which kept them from boarding it or leaving, but it also protected the ship from exterior kinetic energy damage, such as when it slammed into the inner bulkhead, collapsing it and causing the blast hatches to drop down.

Now they were cut off from the rest of the ship. But the damaged wall spilled larval Interlocutors which soon surrounded them. Wiglaf expended the plasma rifle without making a dent, but Magico, seemingly invisible thanks to their feces all over his face, waded amongst them and nipped off their heads with the Interlocutor's pincers like a gardener pruning roses.

"Captain Chrome," the voice of the Interlocutor boomed out over the speakers, "I think now would be an excellent time to reopen our dialogue."

"Nope," Callista said. Twirling and jerking the joystick savagely forward, she made the *Barracuda* turn a cartwheel and smash into the outer bulkhead. "Can't talk if you don't have any air…"

"Oh for fuck's sake, Captain," Skink moaned, "not again…"

"Skink, grab the mummy."

"Why me?"

"Because I hate you most."

The starfish lurched and threw out its arms, suction feet questing for something to cling to, fusion thrusters burping impotently in the tractor web.

"Everybody take a deep breath, hold it, and then blow it all out… now."

The outer bulkhead cracked and tore, and whatever conduit powered the static barrier, life support and the tractor beam relays abruptly gave up the ghost. With a backwards plosive *baba-ka-THOOM* that ended in crackling vacuum, the starfish and all its crew were sucked out into the void.

Kicking and flailing as the last fleeting gasps of air turned to glassy snowflakes all around her, Callista threw her arms wide and trusted in physics to put the starfish between her and deep space.

Now was a terrible time to recall that she flunked physics.

7

Tumbling through vacuum without her shield, hearing only the agonizing voiding of her ears, Callista shut her eye, kept her limbs relaxed and prepared to catch the ship, which was a wall of granulated, horny orange. She judged her velocity with C- aplomb, but after she closed her eyes, *Barracuda* flung out its arms in alarm to grab the walls of the cargo bay. Callista hurtled into the flank of one enormous arm at high velocity, smashing an outstretched arm in a wicked compound fracture, then skipping off the skin of the starfish, unable to grab a handhold, heading for the greedy blackness—

The blackness bit her.

Blackness had white teeth.

She lashed out at the biter and was whipped around, slammed into the starfish again before she realized Lilith was saving her. Stupid dog dragged her the length of the arm and into the oral airlock by her broken arm, only letting go to push the decompression pad with her stupid nose.

Callista used the first burning breath of air to reach her lungs to order a bloody Mary and some painkillers from the replicator.

"Where the fuck is everybody?" she demanded on the comms, when she was halfway through her second drink.

"*Magico, Wiglaf the Incontinent—ow!—and your humble servant accounted for. Also, the fucking mummy.*"

The smashed bones and exposed marrow caught her eye and her nose, already on guard for unpleasant odors, and nearly cost her her drink. "Well done, Mr. Skink. I'll grant your fondest wish on the day after your death."

"You remembered!"

"*Make me into a cushion for your chair, milady.* I'll put it on my to-do list for tomorrow." Leaning on Lilith, she pushed off the outer hatch and weaved through the inner airlock door, cradling her shattered arm.

"Whoever gets to the bridge first, and gets us the fuck out of here under full acceleration scores a weekend of shore-leave…"

"*With you?*" Wiglaf chirped hopefully.

"Wiggy," Callista sighed, "it was sweet, really. But it's over. Don't do it for me, do it so we don't all die."

"*Ugh,*" Wiglaf grunted. "*Will do, anyway.*"

Skink came into the wardroom smoking a fat blunt, only to find a brawny blond lad double-fisting carbo-paste straight from the replicator.

"Watch you don't overdo that shit," he offered helpfully. "It *is* literally recycled shit, after all. Probably been through each of us a hundred dozen times." Then, rubbing his eyes, he thought to ask, "Who the fuck are you, by the by?"

"I'm Poul," said the strapping young lad, staring at the first mate's head, which was draped with fat, pulsing pink and black lampreys.

Skink looked closer, shook his head and said, "Well, don't think I'm cutting you a new belt buckle…"

Poul kept eating, watching the things on his head. Skink

watched him, crossing off the first nine or ten remarks that sprang to mind. Finally, he said, "Look, I know the Captain can be hard cheese, but if you think turning yourself into a man will get you off the hook with the rest of us, you overestimate our standards."

"What do you mean?"

Skink sat beside Poul and offered him the blunt, which he awkwardly accepted. "What exactly do you think space pirates do, love?"

Poul took a tiny hit and broke out in a ripping coughing fit. Mucus jetted out his nose. His eyes practically melted. "I dunno… rape and pillage, I suppose…"

Skink took the blunt before Poul could drop it. "Right, but only on holidays. Just like you join the cops so you can stitch up innocent geezers, but you find yourself eating bad takeout in cars and pissing in soda bottles, waiting for the chance to just fucking shoot innocent geezers, in between the raping and pillaging, there's endless weeks and months of nothing to do but get off your head on drugs, or fuck each other. And we've all fucked each other."

"I'm not here to rape or pillage. I just want to go home."

"Well, like it or no, this here's home, now. And if you think I've been a nuisance, wait'll Wiglaf gets a load of you in that beefcake kit. She'll yank your crank so hard, you'll be pissing through a straw for a month."

"You people are so hard. Is it because you lost your planet?"

"Naw, I'm not from Earth." Skink stubbed out the blunt and pocketed it. Smoke leaked out the corners of his mouth and a loose seal in the top of his skull as he talked. "Somewhere way better. Planet Grime is like Earth, but totally hardcore.

"See, these alien geezers who were scarfing up Earth culture picked up real quick that the best music, jokes and whatnot came from the most oppressed races and classes. Twist the pig's ear, hear him sing, innit? And they figured they could do a better job of it, so they abducted a lot of us and set up a ghetto planet.

"Sort of like a big livestock operation, but with tower blocks, 99% unemployment, gang warfare, sneaker riots, and the presidency was decided by a rap battle. Sickest beats and dopest rhymes in the universe, but then one day, we went too far.

"We launched a real revolution and overthrew our alien overlords. We were finally free."

"That's wonderful."

"You'd think, but no, it was the end. Within a few years, we was all golfing and tying sweaters around our necks and hanging geezers who wouldn't pull their pants all the way up. It was worse than the ghetto, so I left."

Realizing that Poul was still staring at the parasites suckling his scalp, Skink said, "Actually, I was always naff at all that shit. Couldn't draw, couldn't rhyme or drop next-level beats. Why I use these… They're oneirovores, innit? They feed on conscious thoughts, like, but you can take one off your dome and put it on another geezer, right, and that second geezer can soak up what the first geezer was dripping, yeah?"

Pinching a particularly bloated lamprey off his scalp, he offered its gasping, radula-lined maw to the disgusted Warpie. "Go on, try it. It's kind of like a song, but like, with colors like a painting and some grim rhythms. Anyway, I thought of it when I was thinking about you, so like…"

Poul grew slightly taller and hairier as he concentrated on eating paste.

"Fine." Skink reattached the lamprey to his head. "Anyway, Earth was never nothing but a brand name to me, but the Captain, it's a sore spot, so I wouldn't be expecting a ride home until she's got her panties out of her crack by doing something really stupid that gets us all killed, first."

"So you're saying I should just lie back and enjoy being hit on, then walked on."

"Naw, I'm saying we've all been through the mill here, you're nothing special, except you are. You're a fucking shapeshifter, love. If you'd just stop being so fucking mental, you'd have this whole ship wrapped around your finger just like you've got the Captain…"

He bit his tongue, but Poul half-changed back to Poly at the words. Flushing like a southern belle, she said, "But the Captain despises me!"

Skink took the blunt, lit it and sucked it until the discretion lobe of his brain blinked and browned out. "She's never that bitchy to anyone, unless she's protecting herself. You made her feel her feelings, love, and she's been hurt worse than all of us in a blender."

"Was it the computer? Was it someone special to her?"

Skink was just pondering how many blunts he'd need to answer that question, when Wiglaf barged in and immediately glommed onto Poul.

"Thank you, Wotan, for delivering unto Wiglaf the sex dwarf of her dreams! By my sword and my sheath, I am your will made flesh!"

"Knock it off, Wiggy. I saw him first, when he was a she. Go on back to the girl, she'll leave you alone. But like… could you do *this*?" Skink took a creased, grubby snapshot out of his wallet.

"Wotan has spoken! Unhand my sex dwarf, or Wiglaf will tell all to your precious peppermill."

"Don't drag *her* into this, she was just a rebound."

"All of you, shut the fuck up," Callista snapped. Sweeping into the wardroom in a fishnet catsuit, thigh-high patent leather boots, a gray Xrulsh-leather cape and her right arm in a cast and Lilith at her heels, she turned the trashy group into a military unit. El Magico popped up from under the table. He had the semi-conscious pharaoh on a leash. Even Poul stood to attention and dropped the flavorless mush he'd been bulking up on.

"Situation is this. We're on the Mercantile's shit-list, we're more valuable as a controlled substance than as sentient lifeforms, our movements are probably being tracked, and we're down a computer, so we're crawling across the ass-end of the universe, and will all die toothless and pissing ourselves before we reach the nearest neutral settlement where we might trade our cargo for a new navigator."

Hearing all this, Poul looked like he was about to cry. Wiglaf clapped him on the shoulder. "Relax, sex dwarf. Others will die, but Wiglaf will protect you."

"Skink, bug report."

"Ship's been scoured from eyespots to anus and as expected, we're buggy as fuck. Malware, tracking devices, wasp nest factories in our gonads, the works."

"But you ripped it all out."

"Course I did. Why I'm here, innit?"

"Excellent. But no progress on the other…"

"Cobbling together a new warp drive out of spare parts ain't going so well. So unless we draw straws to see who gets to jack in as the new computer…"

"It won't come to that," the Captain snapped. "We'll go to Earth Classic©."

"But that's halfway across the fucking galaxy!"

"Not by wireless. We'll get the best price for our cargo there, and I know Squeers will get us a virtual nav in return for the scanned specs on the neo-Egyptian shit. He's just going to flood the market with cheap copies, anyway."

"So, with the narcs out burning down all humans and the Mercantile hot on our asses, we're going to downcast to the intergalactic clearinghouse for human sleaze to try to beg for a new nav computer, which will come to us via the same buggy wireless channel that turned our replicator into a fucking bug-factory."

"Neatly summarized, Skink, thanks."

"But I skipped the juiciest bit. Because downcasting a virtual nav won't do us no good, unless we have something— or someone—to run it. So the question remainsof who gets the duty—or *what*, I should say, 'cos once they've read the book, they're gonna be a *what*, not a *who*."

"We'll figure that out when we have to, won't we?"

Everybody looked at everybody else. "So who gets to go to see Platypussy?" Skink asked.

"This is not a shore leave. It's going to be all business. Except for you, Wiglaf. This counts as your shore leave."

"Fuck Wiglaf's life," said Wiglaf.

8

Shkasquax XVII's native sentient species are uncannily, if not genetically, identical to Earth's duck-billed platypus, a similarity which has given rise to many Shkasquaxian cults which venerated Earth's monotreme population as a lost tribe. Perhaps it was this bizarre twist of convergent evolution that drove Shkasquax XVII to become so deeply fascinated with Earth that it remade itself into Earth Classic©, an amusement park version of the original. Or maybe they just saw a shit-ton of profit in it.

The result was like one of those weird nobodies who become famous for dire surgical attempts to make themselves into a clone of a famous celebrity, but that didn't stop it from becoming one of the most popular tourist traps in the universe, or an intergalactic clearinghouse for human artifacts, the market for which, Callista figured, would be going out of its fucking mind with the latest news.

She was right. The backlog to downcast into Earth Classic© ran six to nine hours, trapped in a virtual waiting room that put the Hollywood sign over the great pyramids, Easter

Island moai on a boundless prairie with whooping Indians hunting miniature brontosaurus, Roman centurions and Nazi stormtroopers waging war on the Vegas Strip.

But once she got to the first data entry kiosk and dropped Squeers' backdoor access code, they were instantly ripped out of their bodies and into android renter vessels, and she was reassured that she'd picked the best place to hide. Everybody in the universe who could afford it came to Earth Classic© to pretend to be human.

Contrary to what a lifetime of shitty TV sci-fi had taught her, aliens almost never, ever looked like oddly pigmented human beings with latex shit glued to their faces. More often, they looked like something from a tide pool or an Italian modernist furniture gallery. Underestimating them was almost inevitable, and deadly.

But here, they had the advantage, where sea cucumbers who bred pet civilizations like ant farms wobbled and fell on their asses trying to figure out how to get about on two skinny legs while operating a phone.

Fully sensory-compatible, the androids relayed every pang of pleasure, every stab of pain, to their users, creating the largest bandwidth hog in the intergalactic wireless network. Looking at each other in the androids they'd drawn, they all shared a good laugh. Callista was Che Guevara, Skink was Jane Fonda from *Barbarella,* and Wiglaf…

"Who the fuck you supposed to be, Wiggy?" Skink asked in his new, bemused sex-kitten voice.

Wiglaf regarded her muppet-orange spray tan, tiny hands, non-Euclidean combover and hideously spongy torso and said, "I want to switch."

Nobody else wanted to switch.

They emerged into a fair knockoff of Times Square, circa 1973. A mob of homeless actors in superhero and historical costumes posed for pictures or offered guide services through Now Yurk outside Grand Central Station. Feeling reckless in her revolutionary body, Callista cut a swathe through the crowd to hail a cab.

The streets and buildings looked pretty much like New York from the movies and TV she grew up on. Everybody was a celebrity, cartoon character or refugee from a glue-sniffing tween's knowledge of history, and souvenir stands selling T-shirts with botched slogans like I FART NEW YORK, ROCK OUT WITH YOUR DICK OPEN and ARBEIT MACHT FRIES.

The slides were the natives' preferred mode of transport, but if you squinted and ignored the chutes sending duckbilled critters everywhere like adorable mail through pneumatic tubes, all you had to deal with was the clumsy translation of Earth culture for alien consumption, and the cars running people over.

Apparently, the biggest attraction for alien tourists in this part of the park was hit and run driving. A limousine jumped the curb and mowed down half a dozen pedestrians right in front of them, sending realistic bloody body parts flying everywhere, then plowed back into traffic with android sluts in prom dresses YOLOing from the open sunroof. A police car with lights and siren blasting went into pursuit but immediately crashed into a fruit cart, a newsstand and two guys carrying a massive pane of glass, then circled back to finish off the limousine's victims.

If you got offed on Earth Classic©, you were just reshuffled back into the waiting room, Skink reminded them. "Think fast, Wiggy," he added, bumping Wiglaf off the curb. She was immediately smashed like a 250-pound tangerine by an ambulance with flamethrowers.

"Wanker!" Callista kicked him in his bountiful, curvy, pre-"Feel The Burn" Workout buttocks. "This was supposed to be her shore leave."

"She hated that dodgy body, anyway. Did her a favor, didni?" Sidling up close to her so his strawberry blonde hair wafted against her black beret. "So now it's a proper shore leave, innit? Let's go put these sazz-wagon bots through their paces, eh?"

Callista smiled, kissed him on the nose, said, "Maybe next time," and shoved him in front of a speeding city bus.

A few blocks off Times Square, the carefully imagineered sleaze subtly gave way to the real thing. Dealers lurking on every brownstone stoop offered her Spice, Nuke, Chew-Z, Can-D, Merge, Slo-Mo, super-crack, bug powder dust and genuine Florida bath salts. A rape-gang of young Goldblums in matching Jughead hats circled her and did a weird *West Side Story* dance routine around her, but when she refused to give her credit card, they declined to rape her.

It was so stupid. If you forked over for the gang-rape, it would just be interrupted by some asshole Charles Bronson-bot, then you'd be tied up for the rest of the afternoon as a hostage love interest. That was the only thing they really got right about Earth. Your fantasies were always at risk of getting eaten by richer people's fantasies.

Finally, the worsening slum ran into a wall beyond which lay a whole other zone, Namland. The entrance was blocked and plastered with signs promising a NEW ATTRACTION COMING SOON! Peeking between the beams, she shivered.

They'd bulldozed the Mekong Delta and froze it over, turning it into a tessellated snowscape of infinite little millponds behind infinite Lutheran churches, and on every frozen pond, a little girl in a red knit cap and a bright blue parka skated round a pond and sprang into the air and landed on her ass.

Jesus, this was getting weird. Callista had passed on the Costello memeory precisely because it was so popular, but secretly found it an oddly touching slice of someone else's life that she felt oddly guilty about violating; but its continued exploitation utterly confounded and ultimately depressed her. But then, she never understood why people play golf, either.

Squatting in the Namland wall's shadow was the office-burrow of Runcible Squeers, dealer in antiquities, commodities and contraband, and the galaxy's nastiest platypus.

Callista breezed through the security checkpoint, where

slamhound sec-bots drew down on her until her access code cleared.

She was whisked through a gallery showroom mimicking a wing of the Louvre, down to the obscene jumble of legendary paintings, sculptures, installations and memorabilia. Most were probably fakes, but she had a keen enough eye for genuine worth to spot more than a few things that should've been destroyed with the Earth—what, was it only two days ago? Would she gradually start to feel a real sadness, or would it just come down on her all at once, bringing her to her knees? Was she still just in shock, or did she really care as little as she'd always told herself she would, if and when her homeworld was blown up?

She'd been gone only ten subjective years, but figured as much as a century has passed back home. Everyone she knew was long dead anyway, and good riddance. *Lord knows I prayed for it enough times even when I lived there*, she thought, *but I never meant it, and I'd take it back—*

Still, it should trouble her for more practical reasons, right now, before she played her cards with Squeers. Either his operation had included massive larceny and counterfeiting on Earth, a Class IV Interdicted World, or he'd had some inside line on the imminent burnination, and had made a whirlwind acquisition tour.

At the back of the showroom, she let herself in through a secret entrance behind a solid gold statue of Saddam Hussein.

"Ah, the notorious Callista Chrome, in my shop! Everyone comes to buy from me, do you see?" Behind a monstrous desk that might've once belonged to J. Edgar Hoover, Runcible Squeers quacked into a headset. "No more time for your irrelevance! Good day to you, sir!"

Whipping off the headset and flinging it away, Squeers slithered off his high stool and waddled across the room to undulate against Callista's sharp, guerilla shins.

"Ah, word of my vast inventory has reached even the great Callista Chrome, yes? Not even the queen of the primate pirates can resist such a grand sale..."

"I'm not here to buy, I'm here to sell."

"Well, I'm afraid my capital is tied up at the moment. As you can see, I've come into rather a lot of new items. Look around…"

Callista grabbed Squeers by the beak and picked him up. "Couldn't help but notice, the Earth also blew up. The narcs just made you a very rich monotreme."

"Please, Callista! I am only a businessman, and this is my business. Yours too, if I'm not mistaken about our long association. We trade in artifacts…"

"I have artifacts for sale."

"As I said, unless they're quite unique…"

"The tomb-hoard of King Tutankhaten CCXII of neo-Egypt VI."

"Not interested. Anyway, if you came to sell, you'd be here in person. Where are your wares?"

"I can send you scans of every item."

"I can't sell scans."

"You can make copies from them. Half the shit in here is a copy."

"Perish the thought! All authentic! All brought back from beyond the Interdiction Zone at horrible risk! I shudder to think what would become of my reputation if I dropped my pants every time some backwater monarch has a yard sale…"

"You drop your pants so early, the crack of dawn is in danger."

It took some doing to make a platypus blush, but she accomplished it. "Callista, you sully my honor…"

"I'll sully more than that, if you don't quit jerking me around. I'm here incognito, and I need a new nav computer."

"Oh, I thought this sounded like a bad deal, but if all you need is a new computer, I'll gladly take the tomb-hoard of King Nobody-Cares that you don't actually have here to sell. Where is it, pray tell?"

Looking round the store as if a giant blinking bug with a microphone for an abdomen might be waiting on the wall, she said, "I'm not at liberty to say. But I can bring you your goods within minutes of downcasting a new computer."

"Sorry, still not interested. And very busy." Crawling back up his stool, he retrieved his headset.

"I also have King Tutankhaten CCXII himself."

"Ugh… Nobody but other humans care about your icky mummified remains."

"He's not dead."

Squeers's tiny beady eyes widened a bit, didn't they?

"He's still alive and has full cognitive function. I know that a whole live human brain is worth its weight in quantum caps right now, so think what the mind of a monarch would fetch. You could sell the rest as a do-it-yourself mummification kit."

Squeers mulled it over. "You never traded in live humans before…"

"I'm desperate, and not too proud to say it."

"Well then…" He spit in his webbed paw and held it out. "I agree to supply a digital nav-comp in return for the neo-Egyptian artifacts… your living Pharaoh… and an amorous encounter with the infamous space pirate Callista Chrome."

"Oh, come on."

"You said you were desperate. I'm only asking, how desperate are you?" Springing from the stool, he went to a niche and activated another secret entrance, this one leading to a swinging bachelor pad with a rotating water bed, a wet bar, a lava lamp and a vintage Earth hi-fi set.

Feeling suddenly awkward and itchy in her Che Guevara body, she went over and looked distastefully at the waterbed, which was, naturally, a steaming pool of muddy water. "Oh, one more thing…"

"Fuck a duck, what now?"

"I'm not spoiling my reputation for sound business sense, just to cavort with a rental android with a weedy beard and shaky ideology." Scuttling to yet another secret entrance, the platypus smacked a biometric scanner with his flat, beaver-like tail, opening a closet to reveal someone lurking inside.

Callista tensed, expecting an ambush, but it was even worse. The android stuffed into the closet was an all-too-perfect replica of her, convincing in every detail, down to her animated tattoos and mirror-silver hair. He offered her a transport cable, watched as she plugged it into the socket behind her left ear.

"Would you care for a drink?"

"Let's get this over with. How long does the downcast take?"

"Given peak hour bandwidth usage and the local trading cycle—"

Che Guevara slumped to his knees. Now in her bootleg bot-body, she slipped off a stiletto heel and tested its throwing accuracy. "How many minutes?"

He did the calculation, the electrophoric sensors in his head eagerly pulsing as he leered at his distasteful doll. "Approximately twelve."

"That's how long you have," she purred in an infuriatingly husky voice three octaves below her own, "to make a woman out of me."

"But my musk glands must be properly stimulated…"

"Then get to stimulating, and start the fucking downcast," she said, kicking the vacant Che Guevara body over and tossing her heels aside.

Smacking his bill disgustedly, he poked and prodded at a workstation carpeted in purple beaver pelt, muttering, "It's running. Happy now? This abuse will no doubt adversely effect the performance of my erection—"

"Your problem," she said, "not mine." Stepping out of her negligee, she sank into the platypus's muddy waterbed. After downing a furious salvo of performance-enhancing drugs, the platypus cued up a Les Baxter record, waddled over to the stepladder and dove in after her.

9

Believe it nor no, Callista went into her tryst with the platypus with some misgivings. Though she loathed her reputation as a promiscuous vixen, she did enjoy sex as much as any man, and wouldn't be shamed out of it. And though this wouldn't be the first time she fucked someone to get what she wanted, almost without exception, all she wanted was to get *fucked*.

Mostly...

Uncharacteristically, this business of mixing pleasure with business left her feeling dirtier than the mud in which she rested, and doing it in a gynoid sex-doll version of herself only made it that much harder to enjoy the experience. And the little guy was kind of cute...

And she had to face it, the fact that he didn't look like anything any sane human woman would take into her bed was almost a perverse enough temptation in itself, to overcome her doubts. She'd done worse with weirder for a lot less... and mostly enjoyed it.

Mostly...

She recalled the Fehyaiyiin flyer who'd carried her up above a cyclonic storm before penetrating her with a slender, gorgeous organ that vibrated and even sang inside her vagina, making a chime of her ecstatic body, sending her ever higher on thrilling, syrupy waves of exaltation, coming closer than any celibate dervish or flagellating pilgrim did, to touching God.

She thought of the Vorzolvark that escaped its containment cell on *Barracuda* while being transported to some gas-giant mogul's private zoo, and sodomized half her crew to death. Unable to hunt down and kill the beast, she had done some homework and learned the rapacious male was in rut, and utterly submissive to its female counterpart, which made the male of the species look like a cuddly hedgehog.

After el Magico synthesized some female Vorzolvark pheromones from tissue samples left in the rectums of its victims, Callista generously applied them to herself and lured the lust-mad abomination to her room, where she raw-dogged the almost disappointingly compliant slime-devil until it huddled in the corner, mewling for a time-out.

So why did *this* one feel wrong?

Anyway, here he came…

Sleek furry body wrapped round one ankle, tickling its way up her leg. She resisted pushing him away, letting the bubbling jets tenderize her artificial muscles, steeling herself for something unpleasant.

When it happened, it was anything but.

His head broke the surface, bill nestled between her comically oversized tits as the flat of his tail spanked her thighs. "I'll bet you didn't know," he said, "that while most isothermic mammalians only have two sex chromosomes, we Shkasquaxians have ten."

"Most impressive," she humored, pressing her breasts together over his bill to entice him, as well as silence the science lecture. Rolling her hips against the eager little body on top of her and the strategically placed bubble-jet underneath her, she flushed with unfeigned excitement. The little perverts who made this android did gooooood.

His tiny hind legs clawed at her inner thighs, scratching her with his venomous spurs, which seemed to be pumping something other than defensive poison. The gynoid vessel seamlessly relayed every infinitesimal sensation, even the alien drug hammering through her "bloodstream." No doubt, the sensors were calibrated to make the most of Squeers's overtures.

Clasping her thighs tight round his wriggling body, she pushed him against her clitoral hood and felt a surprise. He was waiting for her to notice. "I've had a few modifications made, to enhance our compatibility."

The exuberant, puppy-like pressure was almost like another platypus sprouting out of the first. With legs spread wide, she guided him inside her, first laughing and then gasping as the penis inflated itself a bit to stretch her walls.

"Whatever you paid for that," she moaned, "you got your money's worth…"

She was in a delicious rolling groove, riding a wave that would soon deliver her to the sunny shores of orgasm. Squeers was lost in bliss, nibbling first one breast, then the other, rasping the tender violet floretsof her nipples with the bony ridges with which he crushed the shells of river-shrimp. For a species that lactated through its pores for its blind, hairless young to lap out of grooves in the mother's belly, human breasts were an irresistible luxury.

When he abruptly convulsed and shamefacedly hid his bill under her left boob, she asked, "Did you come already?" She felt a weird weight on her leg, and her rhythm was shattered. "Squeers, did you just *shit* on me?"

"I told you," he quacked, "our sexual composition is… complicated."

She reached down into the hot waterbed and brought up a soft, leathery gray egg. "Oh Squeers, that's adorable… but if this thing looks like me when it hatches…"

"Relax," he told her, rearing up off her bosom and reasserting a confident stroking rhythm. "I eat them every morning... to increase... aaaaahhh... my... potency..."

Now she wanted to keep one, but she had nowhere to stash it, and no way to get it offworld. She let it fall in the water and pressed the platypus down against her, widening her legs to push all of him into the furnace burning inside her.

"I'm so close, Squeers, yes, that's so good... so good, so—WHO THE FUCK'RE YOU?"

A severe-looking man with a long gray beard in medieval clerical robe and a flat hat with a chinstrap stood in the open doorway with a camera out, busily snapping pictures. "Pretty sure I lost the pool, but it'll be worth it when the crew sees this..."

"Skink, get the fuck out of here!"

"But milady, this extravagance of iniquity is man's natural state, if one be not of the Elect... Fuck, I should turn the character feature down..."

Sinking down in the muddy water up to her shoulders and cradling Squeers protectively, she said, "Who're you supposed to be?"

"Do you not recognize John Calvin, the French firebrand of the Reformation, who gave his name to a particularly austere Protestant sect which embraced the predestination of all things? Did you pay attention to nothing in school, Captain?"

She flipped him off. "Go wait outside."

"Ooh, right. Guess who I saw in the waiting room?"

"Just tell me."

"Guess."

"The Interlocutor."

"How'd you know?"

"Because he's hunting us, maybe?" She gave the platypus, still manfully straining to no great effect between her legs, a gentle tug on his pelt. "Time's up, Squeers. The mood is blown, anyway..."

Squeers blew bubbles between her breasts. Squirming out

of her grip, he said, "Something's wrong, my darling… with the Jackrabbit."

"The what?" A flash went off. "Skink, so help me, if you don't stop taking pictures…"

Suddenly, a gloomy, frog-faced philosopher with a lazy eye and black suit flecked with cigarette ashes swept into the doorway with a devastating flying kick that whipped Skink's android head halfway off its ermine-trimmed collar. "Tell Wiglaf, John Calvin. Was THAT predestined? *Was it?*"

Callista lifted Runcible Squeers off her and realized, right away, that something was really, really wrong. She held the platypus up in front of her, thirty-odd pounds of dripping, thrusting duckbilled river-rat.

But she still felt him inside her.

A little bit of blood trickled from a fresh surgical scar in the monotreme's groin, from which a couple loose fiber-optic cables dangled.

"Oh fuck me running," Callista said. "Oh Jesus dick-bananas."

John Calvin and Sartre were still wrestling in the atrium, rolling across the floor clouting each other with Cristo umbrellas. "Stop that," Squeers squawked, "you're ruining my stock!"

"Your stalk is pretty much ruined," Callista said, climbing out of the waterbed. "You wanna get it out of me now?"

"Perhaps now, I have your undivided attention," the Interlocutor boomed from the depths of her uterus, using her cervix as a sounding-board.

Callista dropped Runcible Squeers and whirled around, looking for an external threat, for the Interlocutor to be anywhere but where she knew it was.

"Get it out of me! Get it out!"

Skink and Wiglaf both took pictures. She slapped the phones out of their hands. "Fuck you both, this isn't funny! It's the fucking—"

Just then, she saw them coming in the front entrance. They

must have hijacked the nearest androids they could lay their claws on, which meant an army of eight-year-old girls in red knit hats and bright blue parkas; but you could tell they were Mercantile, because they marched like little girls used to having a huge, trailing abdomens, as if each had a huge load in her snowpants. And all of them were carrying plasma blasters.

Squeers's slamhounds unloaded mercilessly on the human wave attack, but abruptly switched sides, hijacked by the Mercantile horde. Wiglaf took cover and started picking them off with an antique carbine rifle, but for every rosy-cheeked moppet she blew away, two more wobbled into the breach on ice-skates. Skink ran for it, disappearing into the mounds of Earth-shit, the fucking coward.

"We have you surrounded," droned the tiresome voice in her vagina.

"Logout! Logout! Logout!" Callista screamed, but nothing happened.

"We've overloaded the planet's bandwidth with our sheer numbers, so there's a four-hour lag on all logouts. Die, and you get reshuffled back to the waiting room, and right back to us—"

Constricting her Kegel muscles as hard as she could, she still couldn't expel the bio-mech platypus penis, but at least she muffled it a little.

Squeers scuttled out from under his desk, running for another secret burrow. Callista stomped on his tail, pinning him to the floor. "Get us out of here!"

"You never said the Mercantile were cut into the deal. All agreements are nullified! Begone from my shop!"

Callista picked him up by the tail and spun him around like a bolo, threatening to toss him among the implacable, identical little girls moving two-by-two to secure the showroom.

As suddenly as something smashing through a wall, something smashed through the wall. A white paramilitary SUV with a massive passenger bubble of bulletproof polarized glass encasing a gaudy golden throne crashed into and upended

Squeers's waterbed.

Gestatorial Perambulator of Pope George Ringo I, A.D. 2019-2020, said a plaque above the ridiculously inflated price tag.

"Come on, you slags," Skink shouted from the cab. His sour Captain climbed in beside him and Wiglaf, with a plasma blaster on each arm, took the papal rumble seat.

Skink hit the gas and the Popemobile careened through the showroom, plasma beams splashing off the glass bubble like strobelights off a disco ball. Wiglaf shoved a barrel through each of the benediction slots and rained hell on the mob of Noreen Costellos blocking their path. With the crushed husks of determined little girls clogging their wheelwells, the last Popemobile swerved out onto the mean streets of Now Yurk.

"What's the plan, Captain?" Skink demanded.

"We can't log out, we can't get out by dying, and there's about twenty million Mercantile drones on our asses. All suggestions cheerfully entertained."

They turned a corner onto Broadway and found themselves stranded in a sea of yellow taxi cabs. Ahead of them, a mountainous NYPD monster truck-tank hove into view and drove up onto the yellow cab-jam. The tank had a cannon. The cannon fired NYPD squad cars, with lights and sirens and screaming cops, instead of shells.

Skink turned them around and hit the gas, taking out his phone. The monster tank was gaining on them. It fired a whole precinct of cop cars, smashing up the facades of the Great White Way with high-velocity late-model Crown Victorias. One of them smashed the glass bubble off the Popemobile, taking Wiglaf out from the waist up.

"You're just making this needlessly expensive," the Interlocutor said.

Callista shook Skink's shoulder. "Who're you calling?"

Smiling like a cat who'd just eaten his owner's face, Skink turned the Popemobile around, heading straight for the grill of the monster truck.

"Customer service? Yes, I'd like to report a stolen credit card…" He rattled off a number and expiration date, then thanked the operator.

Callista screamed, "What the fuck're you doing?"

Cop cars screaming past overhead, they hit the monster tank head on. The explosion instantly annihilated their android bodies, but they were already gone.

Callista whipped out of her hammock, ripped the VR helmet with all its relays off, and puked all over the deck of the *Barracuda*.

"Pretty clever, yeah?" Skink said, already brushing the vomit out of his gold-plated grill.

Callista came over and planted a sweet, wet kiss on his lips. "That's for saving us." Then she socked him hard enough that he swooned and landed in her vomit.

"And that's for using my card."

10

The sad truth about the life of a space pirate, glamorized in songs, holovids and M'lebomkitari olfactory operas, is that most of it is as boring as anyone else's, perhaps more so, especially once you're tired of fucking each other.

The *Barracuda* limped on through the interstellar void at a paltry third of light speed on a dead reckoning course for the nearest inhabited system. With luck on their side as never before, they hoped to reach it unambushed in a subjective three hundred years.

After their narrow escape from Shkasquax, the Captain showered her crew with drugs and encouraged them to party themselves into a stupor. The next watch, when all were still throbbing with suitably stupefying hangovers, she called a meeting to discuss their situation.

They were a hundred light years from anywhere and highly unlikely to escape Mercantile sweepers, which would pinpoint their location the moment they logged onto the wireless. And while they had the software necessary to get them anywhere in the universe, they still lacked a computer to run it or the means to build one. The only alternative, which no one wanted to suggest, was to upload the navigation software into the only computers they had on hand, their own drug-addled, selfish brains, which could, under el Magico's special care, take them anywhere in the universe with a puff of smoke.

The first option, unanimously approved, was to do it to the pharaoh, but somehow he got wind of what they were planning and fled the cabin with the rest of the crew in hot pursuit, successfully barricading himself in the cargo hold containing his burial hoard. Ever the voice of pragmatism, Wiglaf observed that maybe a brain shaped by two hundred and twelve generations of "true inbreeding" might not be the best vessel in which to entrust their lives.

They reconvened and debated drawing straws, when Skink noisily stopped sipping his own cerebrospinal fluid and made the suggestion they were each fervently hoping someone else would offer.

"Why don't you just do what you did last time, Cap'n?"

Callista broke a bottle over the first mate's head and tried to scrape his face off with the jagged neck. It took the whole crew to pry her off, but she suddenly went limp and dropped the bottle, then stormed off to her cabin, where she remained holed up a month later, when Poly was deputed as a search and rescue party.

Skink had his head in a VR rig and was strapping on a teledildonic suit, so was impatient with Poly's questions.

"Someone's got to go in there, love. We're all starving, since her nibs is hogging all the replicator paste to make her damned fuck-toys, or whatever. Someone's got to go recycle 'em."

"What Wiglaf would not give," Wiglaf lamented, "to eat one meal that has not been inside Captain's holes."

"Why are you all afraid to go in there? What's going on?"

Wiglaf and Skink looked at each other. Lilith got up and padded out of the room with her sleek fur horripilated in glossy spikes.

Not for the first time, Poly worried they were going to grab her and shuck out her brain to use for a new computer, but the two of them did rock-paper-scissors and Skink lost.

"She'd skin me alive if I said anything, but you may as well know.

"The Captain's brooding, but she knows the only way out of this is the worst way, the way she had to do once before.

"See, that computer we had that she had to put down…"

"Was it a friend of hers? A lover?"

"No, you daft Warpie," Skink said, "it was her baby."

Poly looked from one to the other in total incomprehension. For Warpies, life was cheap and short, and love, even between mother and child, all but unheard of. Perhaps that was what made her a mutant like the rest of this crew, she thought. Perhaps she belonged in this sick sideshow.

Skink feigned ignorance of her ignorance for as long as he could, but when he found her stepping on the cord to his VR rig, he reluctantly explained.

"See, the Cap'n came from a planet tougher than any you've ever been to. It's a prison colony on a snowball overrun with bloodthirsty predators. And worst of all, the males and females are from different species, and fuck, do they ever hate one another, and themselves. Rape is a fucking spectator sport, and all the children are bastards. She escaped on a Gray flying saucer that was cruising for slaves, but she turned on them, crippled the ship and slaughtered 'em all… except for el Magico, who told her the only way out was to build a space-warping computer out of the only thing they had ready at hand… her unborn child.

"Them Grays were perverts, but they were onto something. See, they knew that the uniquely fucked structure of the human brain allows it to cook up hypothetical situations so vivid, it forgets which is which, and it fucks off right across time and space, and takes us with.

"The Cap'n, she didn't give a fuck about much even then,

but she loved that baby, maybe for the pain she went through to get it. She didn't take the decision lightly, and since then, she's been diamond-hard. She knows it's the necessary, if we're ever getting out of here. Three hundred years in deep space with no downloads, the same recycled food, the same wack porn..."

Poly blinked. "She's not the only female onboard. Why don't one of us do it?"

Wiglaf shook her head. "Wiglaf is only nine. First period not for another year, maybe two." The barbarian had spent her downtime battling hologram enemies in her bunk, and her skin was a patchwork of fresh scars and bulging veins. "Soon, must build first menstrual hut, make blood-offering to Wotan."

"But..."

Wiglaf shook her head. "Must be someone Captain trusts, even loves. And there is no other."

"What planet does she come from, that made her so hard?"

Skink looked left and right. The word, spiky and cold, fogged his breath as he whispered it. "Alaska."

"Pshaw," Wiglaf spat. "Is nowhere near as terrible as Warworld III."

"Says you," Skink scoffed. "You wouldn't last a second against those, what did she call 'em, those *moose* motherfuckers? You'd run home crying to your precious Warworld, with an antler up yer arse..."

Poly took the replicator's telescoping disposal intake and fled the room with the hose dragging behind her, trying to keep her goosebumps from evolving into screaming mouths.

She vacillated for an immeasurable interval before the Captain's door with her hand poised to knock. When she finally got up the nerve, Callista's voice snapped, "Come in, then, damnit." The door whisked open and the pile of food trays and broken sex toys spilled out into the corridor.

Callista Chrome reclined on her bed with a cigarette in a long holder and a tattered xenobiology catalogue and an overflowing ashtray on her knees. Clad in satin pajamas, her trademark hair dyed deep purple-black, she'd put on some weight. Her perky breasts had acquired a robust, pouty fullness, her deep purple nipples wept. Her pale, dusky skin gleamed with hormones, her unkempt hair shone and wafted a spice on the air that stirred Poly's own sex, so she had to struggle not to revert back to Poul as she stooped to pick up the mess.

Each broken dildo, tickler and string of anal rosary beads she collected was more outlandish, intimidating and exotic than the last, until she recoiled in terror from a biomechanical phallus that yawned and flashed rows of steel teeth and oozed protoplasm in her hand.

Poly shuddered as she dropped the horrid thing into the disposal hose. "You… put this inside you?"

"Just fucking the pain away, baby," the Captain said. "You ever see a movie called *Alien*?"

Poly nodded out of habit, but then shook her head, deciding not to ask what a movie was.

"I'll show it to you sometime, when we're not blacked out. I swear, the first time I saw that shit… I was twelve. I was just starting to feel horny, but the boys in town were all so gross and stupid, I couldn't believe what I was feeling was for them. It had to be something more, and none of the girls wanted to play my games…

"Then I stayed up late one night and saw this old movie… I couldn't believe they showed it on basic cable, it was almost the most hardcore porno I'd ever seen. Almost…"

Clearly aroused by her own story, Callista gently rocked her pelvis and oscillated her hips, working herself into a wistful frenzy.

"They called the thing a monster, but right away, I knew what it really was. It was *sex*—pure sex incarnate, harder than steel and softer than velvet, and it wasn't eating the stupid human crew, it fucked them with its tongue because they wouldn't just get down with it.

"At the end, when the final girl confronts it in the space shuttle, you think they're going to drop the horror bullshit. When

Ripley strips and she's all, 'Lookit my boobs,' and the xenomorph is all, 'Check out my mouth-dick,' you think it's going to be the hottest fucking sex scene in the history of cinema…

"I came for the first time just watching, it was so fucking hot… but then they blew it. Watching that scene on DVD was a huge disappointment, too. I figured they must've cut out the best part, but no such luck. I rubbed my clit raw just pausing and backing up every time Ripley chickens out.

"I knew then, I wasn't going to find what I wanted on my home planet… Oh for fuck's sake, what's your problem?"

"I'm sorry, Captain…" Poly had warped into a fair approximation of the monster from Callista's old movie, albeit with a fierce rack of moose antlers, and the fanged tongue dangling from between her shiny biomechanical legs. Tears of slime wept from it and in a tiny, mucus-choked voice, it whimpered, "Why do you hate me?"

"I don't hate you, but you never stand up for yourself. I can't have one of my crew going all moony and, *I'm Sorry* every time they fuck up, or someone knocks them down."

"I wish I was strong, like you…"

"Strong!" Callista spat the word out and wiped her tongue. "You know what people who've been through hell hate being told? That they were strong. 'Strong' implies that they had the muscles to take it, that it was easy, just another workout, thank god you're so strong. What it takes to get through what we've all been through, you don't know you have it until your muscles have given out. You've got muscles to spare, but you don't have any idea what 'strong' really means, honey."

"May I ask a question?"

Regarding her with a flicker of momentary intrigue, the Captain said, "You may."

"How much of your abuse must I cheerfully bear, if I'm not worthy of your love."

"Sucks when you put it that way, but since you put it that way…"

"But I can become anything you want…"

"That's just it, dear," Callista said, kicking a few more broken sex toys out of her bed. "Do I look like a girl who knows what she wants?"

"You wanted… to fuck the alien…?"

"I always wanted to meet aliens, sure. Real spacemen, you know? Maybe because everybody I knew on earth was an asshole. But all I've found out here is just new and different kinds of asshole, and I have to wonder… are they assholes just like us, or are they assholes *because* of us?"

"Maybe that's all you found," Poly said, "because that's all you were looking for." When the Captain didn't haul off and slap her, Poly reached out and touched her arm, murmured, "You want a child… I could give you…"

Callista ripped her arm free. "Fuck out of here, with your ideas about what I want. You want to know what I want? When I've got one in the oven, when it's viable, I'm going to extract it and implant it in an artificial womb, and then freeze it… then I'm going to download the navigational backup into my own brain."

Poly gasped in shock so profound her antlers fell off. "But you'll… that will be the end of you!"

"That's what I want, stupid girl."

"But why? You have everything, you… you…"

"I've *had* everything, and it wasn't enough to make me forget, let alone make me happy. I'm over it, all of it. I've been playing this stupid pirate game so long, I don't remember what winning was supposed to look like. But just folding and not having to fight, not having to feel anything anymore… that feels like winning, right now. Maybe my child will do it better than I did, and find better games to play."

"You could still change. Only love and death offer us the chance to be better…"

"I don't want to be better, I'm not afraid of death, and I don't love you. Any more bright self-care suggestions? I'm all ears, doll."

Why was her heart so tightly bound to this miserable creature, so intent on her own end? Perhaps because she could never save her, she thought, because it was the most exquisite punishment she could foist upon herself, for her own sins.

Still in her biomechanical incubus form, Poly swept up the rest of the flotsam and jetsam of the Captain's solo orgy in sullen silence.

"Get lost." Callista busied herself modeling a Fomalhautian chimera's mating prong for the replicator. "And tell Skink to take a shower and come make me a baby."

11

The decision to spawn a new quantum uncertainty computer from her own loins was not an easy one, but Callista Chrome knew there was no other way out. Even with hormonal rejuvenation treatments, her crew wouldn't last another seventy-three hours, let alone years, before someone pieced together the dismantled communicator and logged on, advertising their whereabouts and helplessness to the Mercantile and every other scumbag in the human-pushing game, creeps from backwater shitholes where Axe Body Spray is a form of currency.

It was so fucking unfair, but she shouldn't have been surprised. In every movie and TV show she ever watched, the humans rose to take their place at the center of the universe, forcing their bilateral symmetry and secular humanism and velour uniforms on all but the scabbiest, orc-like alien races. Aliens more advanced than humanity should be like God was supposed to be, inscrutable but ultimately wise and benevolent.

To find that aliens were at once every bit as crass, vulgar and violent as the morons back home was a hard blow; but to find that in the galactic scheme, humanity was at best a pest and at worst a dangerous controlled substance, to be consumed by degenerates or destroyed without remorse by puritanical assholes, and all because of the same capacity for imagination that led humans to reach out to those ungrateful fucking freaks, was enough to make her regret bothering to leave home.

Worst of all, it shouldn't be this boring.

The first time she saw another town, she didn't know what to expect, but was inconsolable when it turned out to be just a similar cluster of convenience stores, gas stations, trailer parks and crappy prefab government buildings, with the same extended cab pickups and lardass SUV's cruising the main drag like ticks on a dead dog's belly. Even worse, the first time she saw another country and found it to be the same old shit, and she despaired of reaching the stars. When that chance came, it turned out to be anything but the miracle she'd prayed for her in her dreams, but she finally let herself believe she'd risen above the garbage-heap of her upbringing, finally escaped into the unimaginable.

But it was more of the same.

Strip malls, casinos, cantinas, arenas and whorehouses: Alaska, ad infinitum. And even worse, with human brains under interdiction, the most grotesque and kitschy parts of human culture and design became omnipresent kneejerk counter-culture statements, and as the universe self-consciously adopted baggy Jinco jeans and extravagantly awful shopping malls, how could she deny that her species was a plague, in need of a genocidal cure?

Interstellar truck stops with ninety-six species of prostitute still smelled like beef jerky farts and meth sweat and desperation, the nightclubs played shit that sounded like Donna Summer filtered through forty-two layers of bad translation, and all her relationships ended the same way, with her pushing away anyone who threatened to become more demanding or risky than her museum of broken sex toys.

She should feel something about this, something more than just the gush of ersatz emotions from the hormones she'd taken to insure proper ovulation. This was the one thing, the only thing, she swore she'd never do again, but even as she reminded herself, she was taking steps to get it over with.

After carefully scrutinizing the crew's dubious DNA, Wiglaf emerged as the runaway favorite, despite the setback of her gender. Callista spiked her morning mush with Denebian slime-angel glandular secretions, a full dose of which would be sufficient to turn her into a male, but the canny barbarian noticed the flavor and fed her portion to Lilith, who became so excitable that she chewed her new penis off and dragged her hindquarters around the ship until her old genitalia grew back.

However she felt about him, el Magico was literally one of the creatures who abducted her and took her baby out of her, and his bedside manner was a stone drag.

Which left Skink…

A knock at her door and the first mate entered, freshly juiced muscles glistening and dripping with shower-gel and six kinds of aphrodisiac. "What is her majesty's pleasure, mum?"

Callista rolled over and drew back the sheets, kicking out empty bottles and trying to stifle a yawn as Skink sloughed off his bathrobe. "Let's just get this over with, OK?"

Gyrating her hips and looking slyly over her shoulder at him, Callista Chrome urged Skink to take her, so he did.

But even as he plunged into her and began thinking of obscure navigational calculations to stave off the inevitable, the teledildonic interface was tugged slurping and gulping off his trembling blue erection.

Holo-goggles stripped off his face, he winced at the light, fully expecting the business. Captain Chrome had deleted the crew's stash of bootleg revenge porn of her, but he'd managed to keep a couple choice encounters from the halcyon first week of his tenure on the *Barracuda*, before she moved on.

That was how Callista Chrome kept her crew together. She seldom fucked any of them more than once, but once was enough to effortlessly command their loyalty, take them for granted and treat them like shit's ginger stepsister, without ever offering the dimmest glimmer of hope of another taste of heaven.

Looking up at her now, he found himself at a loss for words. She smirked at the tinny, beckoning succubus in the VR rig, then took hold of his organ with a simmering stare like a lioness defending a not-quite finished kill.

"Cap—that is, your Majesty, I—"

She put one gloved finger to his lips. "Ssssshhh," she said. "Don't turn this rape into a murder."

Lowering herself onto Skink's cock, she moaned deeply with each peristaltic gulp, clenching him and then widening her hips until she had him completely engulfed.

Try as he might, even Skink's basic multiplication tables eluded him. His hands came up to caress her breasts, but she batted them away. "Don't touch me," she husked. Her eyes slitted, her breath hot, pheromone-laced mist on his face, driving him so crazy with arousal that he snarled and snapped at her, biting her shoulders and neck.

She pinned his arms behind his head and hunched over him like a jockey driving a thoroughbred. She bit his throat just hard enough to pinch shut his carotid artery, while at the same time spurring the blood from his femoral artery into his cock, which became super-engorged, doubling in girth at the cost of bloodflow to his brain.

Skink spasmed under her, finally giving her the release she chased. Her moans of pleasure became howls of abandonment, both exultant in fleeting freedom, and mournful in grasping the coattails of death.

Long after she recovered, she wrenched her pelvis against his in a deliberate milking rhythm, eliciting gasps of delirium from her helpless prey. Like a spider wrapping its next meal, she lifted herself off him and reattached his teledildonic appliance, zipped him into his suit and slipped the goggles back over his unseeing eyes.

Time passed.

The *Barracuda* painfully crawled across the black face of infinity. The crew, each in his or her own way, went a little mad.

The Captain continued her lonesome vigil, consuming as much of the ship's scant, oft-recycled resources as before, but at least eating it.

Wiglaf trained, Skink wanked, el Magico meditated, Lilith brooded outside her master's door, and Poly tried to stay out of the way, for the next six months.

Until one sleepy third watch, when Callista came onto the bridge with her suede flightsuit unzipped to set free her bulging second-trimester belly. "Let's do this."

Wiglaf and el Magico looked at the deck. "Captain sure she wants to go through with this…?" El Magico wheeled out the artificial womb with a big DO NOT EAT sticker on the side and skinned his enormous, spidery hands into thick rubber gloves. "Can have another baby, but…"

"You're right… I changed my mind," Callista said.

Now they looked at each other. This shit was clearly a trap. "But Captain," Wiglaf sputtered, "you said—"

"Now I'm saying, Just get it out of me, upload the backup, and get us the fuck out of here. And *now* is who I am."

Callista climbed into her egg chair and reclined with her legs akimbo, unzipped the crotch of the flightsuit until her inflamed vagina was completely exposed. El Magico laid his clinically unimpeachable hands on Callista, staring searchingly into her eye until she growled at him to get on with it. Then he broke out a fluorescent mushroom cap from his medicine bag and gave it to the Captain to chew. Within minutes, she went into labor.

El Magico guided the unripe fetus out of the birth canal and delicately inserted his fingers to cradle the head as it emerged, still swaddled in a pulsing amniotic sac. Twisting and turning the unfinished fetus until the placenta came completely free, he snipped and capped the umbilical cord, then plugged the cord into the socket on the incubator. Then, after another long staring battle with the Captain, he reached over and hit the Enter button on the nearest terminal.

Lights dimmed throughout the ship, then surged brighter as the computer began to actuate and take command of the ship's functions.

Wiglaf and Magic high-fived and were just settling down with a spliff and a tankard of ale when Captain Callista Chrome strode onto the bridge with her protruding belly parting the folds of her feather robe. "Blast that traitorous Warpie cunt out the fucking airlock, right now."

Wiglaf did a spit-take. El Magico did a face-palm and swallowed the joint.

"You're too late." The other Callista Chrome closed her legs and zipped up her flightsuit, hugging her deflated belly and staving off creeping, crippling gloom.

El Magico blew smoke into the intake ports on the artificial womb, now the universe's most powerful and unpredictable form of propulsion.

"All systems online, Captain," Wiglaf said. "Engaging the quantum uncertainty drive."

Callista seized her doppelganger by the lapels and hauled her out of the captain's chair. "What the fuck have you done?"

"I saved our child... saved you," Poly answered, letting the disguise fall away, but revealing only another disguise. Nobody knew what a warpie's true form was.

"Unplug that monster..."

"It's still Skink's baby..."

The first mate poked his head into the bridge. "Nobody can prove nothing!"

"This bitch used you to make herself a baby, now it's in charge of the ship..."

"It's just a computer now," Poly mewled. "Just what you wanted."

"Wait, when did this happen? When did she and I... Oh fuck, that was... Hold up..."

"You thought it was just another holo-wank session," Poly said with grim satisfaction. These people weren't so smart, after all.

Callista shook her head, pulled her hair into spikes. "If Skink and I never... then *you* came in my room, as Skink... and this..." She grabbed her belly.

Poly cried, "I just wanted... to share that with you." She lay weeping inconsolably on the deck at the Captain's feet, praying to be spared and hoping they'd carry her off and blow her into the void, just get it over with.

"Fine," Callista Chrome said, biting the fingertip of one crushed-velvet glove and ripping off one, then the other. "Do whatever you want. Magico, get this parasite out of me and into the freezer. Wiglaf, plot a course for Warworld III. First sign of insubordination, burn it."

"Ah... Warworld III... Wiglaf thinks you should know..."

"Shut up, Wiglaf." Callista lounged in the chair and let el Magico extract the half-Warpie fetus while she lit and put out a series of cigarettes. "They're going to track us, if they can, trying to find the last human enclaves. If someone's following us, they're going to regret it when they get where we're going."

"But Captain..."

"I said, Shut up, Wiglaf."

"But what about this one?" the barbarian pointed at Poly, who still cowered on the deck.

"Confine her to quarters. If she's hungry, let her eat that." The Captain kicked the side of the incubator with their baby in it, and ordered el Magico to fuck them off to Warworld III.

"How can you be so cruel?" Poly wailed as Wiglaf hauled her away.

"That part's easy, honey," the Captain replied with a desolate, lopsided smile. "We're the scum of the Earth."

13

WARWORLD III is a dumping ground (and breeding ground) for humanity's absolute worst, and has existed in a state of constant warfare for centuries... a furnace visited only by those seeking the fiercest berserkers in the known universe for televised gladiatorial warfare.

As such, it was perhaps the only place fugitive humans could throw off any less-than-fanatical pursuit, though all but a foolhardy few chose quick death in space over whatever fate awaited them beneath Warworld III's perpetual shroud of nuclear winter clouds.

But even the most astrophysically illiterate twit in the galaxy probably could've told you that the planet they were orbiting was not Warworld III.

"Fuck is that pitiful shitball?" Callista spat, surging out of her chair towards the monitor as if it had called her fat.

"Erm," Wiglaf grumbled. El Magico lit another joint and planted a solid kick in the guts of the incubator. "Must've made mistake..."

The planet beneath them was a mottled green toroidal body with 58% of Earth's mass, circling a white dwarf star amid an alphabet soup of similarly unlikely asteroids. An arboreal doughnut-world of skyscraping jungles broken by shallow, asparagus-green seas and swampy daiquiri ice glaciers at its poles, it had a gleaming flying fortress in stationary orbit at the center of its doughnut-hole, out of which wave after wave of manned blastboats came screaming in their direction.

"Blastboats?" Callista scoffed. "Fucking seriously?" Whoever was oppressing the Warpies, they had their callous-disregard-for-life game down pat. Little more than rocket-driven bobsleds with minimal maneuvering capability, blastboats carried disposable marines onboard in the unlikely event the missile hit anything that could be taken by force, so they were first and foremost a good way to get rid of surplus cannon fodder.

Callista cracked open an amyl nitrate vial under her nose and inhaled violently, dancing in place as she rattled off orders. "Battle stations. Warm up the gonads. Deploy nano-chaff. Arm meat-seeking missiles. See if you can make that little bastard evac us to where I told it to take us. And get that two-faced bitch out of her cabin."

"Why, Captain?" Wiglaf said.

"She hijacked us," Skink said, "her and her chappie." Crooking a trembling finger at the monitor, he added, "That's Warpworld, innit?"

"Is not freak's fault," Wiglaf said. "Captain, Wiglaf must confess—"

At that moment, a death ray slashed through the bridge of the *Barracuda*. For all intents and purposes, the beam was simply there and then not, leaving a gaping hole in the bulkhead and decapitating Wiglaf as neatly as a guillotine, but Callista could've sworn that Wiglaf was already in motion when the beam penetrated the ship.

The bridge explosively decompressed. Skink stayed strapped to his console. Callista sprang at the rip, catching

Wiglaf's severed head like a football and deployed her magnetic boots to bring her indelicately but securely onto the edge of the rip. El Magico surfed the hurricane of cargo containers, blowup dolls, pony kegs, hookahs and sundry other appliances of pirate life, all the while herding the flying junk into such a shape that it blocked, at least temporarily, the rip in the flesh of their starfishship. Only Wiglaf's headless body tumbled out into space before the wounded *Barracuda* began to heal itself, sealing the wound with a gusher of quick-congealing blood.

The bridge repressurized almost as violently as it was emptied. Under the Captain's arm, Wiglaf mouthed a mute apology.

But they were still under attack. The *Barracuda* had foxed most of the hapless blastboats with automated defensive measures, but now scores of the assault craft circled the embattled starfish, harrying its spiny endodermis with fusion beams to keep it pinned down until the flying fortress's death ray could be deployed again.

Before even the speed-jagging Captain could order it, el Magico went to the incubator and whispered into its vents, curls of feathery golden smoke emitting from his lipless mouth.

A moment of pure vertigo, their eyes pressed back in their sockets and limbs swelled up to fill every cubic inch of the bridge...

And then they were back in objective space and out of whatever void they fell into when their unborn navigator got too high to remember where they were.

"Goddamnit, Magico..." Callista flung her hands up in despair. "Why don't any of you fucking pirates follow orders?"

They had dropped from their location in outer Warpworld orbit like a forgotten court date, only to emerge at the same instant a mere couple hundred thousand kilometers away, almost quick enough to see their own stern vanish in a cloud of golden smoke.

They emerged literally on top of the flying fortress. The *Barracuda* deployed its suction cups and attached itself to the hull of the fearsome orbital weapons platform like any terrestrial starfish opening an abalone shell.

Despite redundant layers of static shields and blowback armor, the flying fortress was not designed to withstand being cracked open by a pissed-off mega-echinoderm, and so gave way with anticlimactic ease, spilling hundreds of thrashing, kicking dying lifeforms and all their personal possessions into the indifferent void like so much piñata candy.

After that, the blastboats veered off and descended to the planet's surface. As the alarms cut off, Callista dropped Wiglaf's head in Skink's lap. "Put this in the freezer."

Skink picked up the head and immediately his mind was overrun with bad ideas. "Why don't we grow her a new body? I could show you a catalogue…"

"Growing her a new body'll take weeks and most of our food reserves. We don't have time."

"Why don't we go find her old body and stitch it back on?"

"It's out there somewhere, flying away at high velocity. We can't spare a crewmember to look for it."

"Why don't we go find it and grow the old head a new body, and grow the old body and new head? Then we'll have two."

"Because we have even less time now, than the first time I said it. Also, the new head would be a fucking infant, with none of Wiglaf's training or personality. It'd just be a big, terrifying sex doll. Why are you fucking arguing with me? Just… freezer… *now*."

Skink hustled off with the barbarian's head. El Magico ushered Poly onto the bridge. The gloomy girl was weeping uncontrollably, but her eyes took on a strange light when she saw her troubled homeworld on the monitor.

"Yeah, your little plan worked. Magico, unplug the warp drive computer and bring me a melon baller. We're going to upgrade the wetware and try again."

Even el Magico balked at this drastic plan. Poly threw herself on the incubator. "You monster! You wouldn't!"

"You can't imagine what I'd do to anyone who threatens

my command." Sharpening a knife, she knelt until she and the Warpie girl who had twice shared her bed were nose to nose. "You dragged us across the galaxy to overthrow your oppressors, but we're not freedom fighters. We don't work for free, and we barely give a fuck away."

Poly's face fell. "Maybe I brought you here to show you you're not the only one who's suffered. Maybe to give you something better to do with your own pain than cut yourself up with it. And maybe to show you that the weakest can rise up…"

Callista blinked and twitched, inhaled another vial. "OK, I apologize. Do you accept my apology?"

Poly stared for a gravid, laborious moment, then nodded.

"Good, we're all friends again, everything's fine." Callista offered her a dazzlingly unconvincing smile. "You know how some breeds of woodpecker can wrap their tongues around their brains when they do their thing?"

Poly arched her eyebrows quizzically. Callista dashed her forehead into the bridge of Poly's nose, crushing it and knocking her out cold.

"God, I wish I could do that," Callista groaned, rubbing her swollen forehead, turned on el Magico. "Get me one of those stupid blastboats and make sure Lilith is up to date on her shots."

El Magico scowled and took off his hat, searching the hatband until he found a pouch of fitfully glowing green powder. Callista slapped it out of his hand, then took out a shock-collar and locked it around Poly's neck. Jerking her upright, the Captain dragged her by a leash to the airlock. "The girl was right. Let's go do some misery-tourism."

The lone blastboat skipped off the canopy of the impenetrable jungle like a stone across a scummy blue-green, bottomless pond, smashing through a swarm of startled arboreal jellies like windblown dry cleaning bags before coming to rest nose-down in the fruiting body of an enormous brain fungus.

Captain Chrome popped the hatch and sprang out of the cramped fuselage, wiping el Magico's dandruff off her blood-red patent leather pressure-suit, polarized bubble helmet and thigh-high steel-toed boots.

Lilith leapt giddily out of the blastboat and squatted to piss, fogging up and licking the inside of her space-helmet. El Magico unfolded himself from the stern of the three-man blast-boat and took out a thing like a set of bagpipes which, naturally, turned out to be another form of hookah, which he plugged into his oxygen tank.

Deprived of all but the dimmest rays of sunlight by the canopy, the undergrowth was almost entirely carnivorous—a neon coral reef of dazzling birdfisher lures, opal-studded sundew anemones, snapping flytrap jaws and simmering pitcher plants that tailored and ratcheted up their pheromone output to entice animal prey to drink deep of their nectar and be digested in ecstasy.

El Magico told the Captain the atmosphere was breathable, but Callista said, "Fuck that shit. Breathable atmosphere is for suckers. Helmets stay on, except for her." She twitched Poly's leash, sending a gentle kiss of voltage to her collar. "It's your home, after all, right?"

Poly jolted to full alertness, her shape going vague with a dozen renegade fight-or-flight forms, until Callista gave her another shock. "What is this? Why am I on a leash?"

"You've been demoted," Callista said, "to a dog."

Noticing how Lilith looked at her with fresh interest, she said, "But I don't want to be a—"

"Heel!" Callista jerked Poly's leash and sent another surge of voltage through her mercurial body. Arching her spine until her feet nearly touched the back of her head, she convulsed so hard she could barely bring herself to submit to wearing a canine shape.

She had chosen a male form compatible with Lilith's to

establish dominance, but the bitch wasn't having it. Poly blocked her mind against a blizzard of telepathic animal nastiness—*Dog rips ears off fake dog/Dog chews off fake dog's legs/Dog grinds her cunt on crippled fake dog's face/Happy Dog!*—instead of keeping her attention where it belonged, on the lady holding her leash.

"Go on," Callista barked, "take me to your leader."

Poly sniffed the perfumed jungle breeze, looked warily at her growling rival, and led them down invisible game trails through the endless jewelry box of man-eating plants. Callista hacked at grabby vines with a pocket chainsaw and decapitated flytraps with a wrist-blowtorch, but suddenly she was being dragged through the overgrowth by Poly, who plunged deeper into the jungle, heedless of Lilith pummeling her flanks with her bubble-helmet, trying to sink her jaws into the Warpie's shape-shifting, electrified flesh.

Despite the pungent miasma of the jungle, long before they laid eyes on what summoned her, Poly and Lilith could smell it, too. The olfactory siren songs and underlying rot of the riotous flora abruptly crumbled under the overpowering stench of burning, the sick-sweet dirge of charred fauna in unspeakable abundance.

Poly dragged her through a curtain wall of spongy fungi and into a clearing, and the Warpie village.

It reminded Callista of Whoville, a charming huddle of bulbous huts and fabulous non-Euclidean temples, magic rock gardens tended by adorable sea monkeys, but something about the ugly burnt umber-maroon-sienna-avocado-goldenrod carpet color scheme made her hate it. It was straight out of Dr. Seuss, right down to the fires, the rampant rape and looting and the hulking saurian brutes wantonly burning down everything that moved.

The Warpies looked like somebody with way too much arts & crafts experience glued googly eyes and glitter to a bunch of disembodied human stomachs. They groveled and crawled and wailed tubercular dirges with boneless tendrils that were both limb and mouth.

"Is that what you really look like?" Callista cackled until her sides hurt.

They were the most piteous creatures ever to kiss a boot, but they got not a moment's respite from their tormentors.

Back when humanity was reduced to heeding the speculations of its nerdiest nerds for insight into intelligent life on other worlds, it was accepted wisdom that any race sufficiently intelligent to develop interstellar travel would be both enlightened in its respect for inferior forms of life, and advanced enough to have no need to exploit or attack other civilizations for material gain. They repeatedly and with great erudition assured themselves that when the aliens came, they would be infinitely more merciful than their European ancestors had been with every other culture they contacted, and wouldn't need to cross light-years of space to take their water or women.

The Monitors were that rare exception that proves those optimistic nerds read entirely too much Asimov, and not enough Ellison.

Whatever immortal hand or eye had lifted these irascible four-eyed lizards onto their hind legs, gifted them with thumbs and fusion drive warships and sent them rampaging through the galaxy like a plague of flaming alley cats into a Manila tenement, it only spared them the same vicious genocidal interdiction that wiped out humanity by denying them our unique gifts for cognitive dissonance and irresistible cultural ephemera.

Callista supposed she was partly to blame for this monstrous auto da fe. No doubt the Monitors were stirred up by the giant starfish that appeared out of nowhere and fucked their orbital fortress to death. But something told her this was just another day in Warpieville.

The Monitors trampling hapless natives wore tunics and bulging codpieces of glittering Pepto-Bismol pink Warpie flesh. When she opened fire on one, Poly howled, and even Callista blanched when she realized what she'd done.

The Monitor's garments were actually living Warpies, tamed and trimmed to fit their enslaver's bodies as both armor and live hostages, becoming glittery mirror-carapaces to deflect energy beams. Even as the Monitors turned from the massacre to lay down a hailstorm of plasma on their would-be rescuers, the enslaved Warpies gave their own lives to protect the scaly skins of their oppressors.

"How do they make them do that?" Callista marveled, looking from the abominable display of dominance to the shock collar holding Poly in check, then back, with an unsettling gleam in her eye. "I've gotta get one of those."

El Magico let her know that their enemies, though arguably less sentient than any Komodo dragon boring the shit out of tourists in an earthly zoo, possessed a crude form of rudimentary telepathy which allowed them to enforce their demands.

"Why didn't you say so?" Callista said, and knelt beside Lilith to remove her helmet and whisper in her ear. The dog whined with eager glee and lunged until she stood up on her hind legs at the end of her sparking, short-circuiting leash.

Even Callista was brought to her knees by the flood of Technicolor canine filth that blasted a two-mile radius with traumatic images and sensations—*Dog at play/Ripping the tails off lizards/Shakes lizards by their wattled necks/Lizard heads crunch/Eyes pop out/Crunch bones/sweet Monitor marrow/Dog drags her diarrhea-ravaged ass on lizard carcasses/Humps severed tails/Happy Dog!*

A couple dozen Monitors staggered and flopped thrashing onto their backs, firing spasmodically into the air as Poly and Lilith scampered among them, ripping out their exposed throats. Callista and el Magico stepped over hyperventilating Warpies to execute the Monitors with their own plasma blasters.

But as Poly raced around the village square, she ignored the surviving Monitors already beginning to recover from the canine mind-meld. Instead, she sank her teeth into and shook the timid, googly-eyed stomach-blobs, flinging them into the air in her desperate ferocity. As they flew, each of them exploded in traumatic transformation, landing on oversized, leathery paws, whipcord tails wagging, jubilantly barking, slavering with centuries of hate and hunger. Before Callista could decide whether this development was an improvement, the square was filled with identical black, yellow-eyed attack dogs.

Together, they made Lilith's dream come true.

Ripping, tearing with teeth and claws, day-glo lizard blood dripping from long muzzles, the dog pack reduced the Monitor horde to bloody bone fragments in less time than it takes to come up with an idea for a new Star Wars spinoff trilogy.

Surveying the hideous carnage and the still more unsettling sight of the bloodthirsty renegade Warpie pack crowding round her and baying at the twin moons, Callista was momentarily at a loss for how to turn the situation to her advantage. Which one was Poly? Why did she want her back?

Turning to el Magico and plugging a cigarette into a special port on her helmet, Callista asked, "I don't suppose there's one central whatever that we can blow up, that'll topple all of them at once?"

El Magico shook his head.

"Fine, we'll do it the Vietnam way." Sucking the cig down to the filter in one breath, she added, "but by this time tomorrow, we'll win."

Looking out over the sea of panting black muzzles and beady yellow eyes, Callista saw a dog wearing a shock collar, pinning down and savagely fucking a whining, yipping bitch in a matching collar. Eyes ablaze with bloodlust that betrayed no splinter of the meek and gentle creature she was before, Poly lifted her muzzle and howled in ecstatic desolation as she came inside Lilith, and Callista's exultation turned to ashes as she found herself feeling jealous of her dog.

14

The liberation of Warpworld, like the Vietnam conflict, ground on for longer than planned on even shakier ethical grounds, with a shitload more casualties. All told, it took a little more than two days (which, on Warpworld, is less than fourteen hours). Lizard after lizard, cow after cow, village after village, they swept in behind a pack of baying telepathic dogs, paralyzing the Monitors and spreading the rebellion until an army of black, bloody hounds surrounded the unlovely compound of mud huts and dropships that comprised the Monitors' planetary stronghold.

It was a pathetic excuse for a spaceport, but more than adequate for fending off a ragtag horde of guerilla fighters whose only ranged weapon was pissing on everything. Automated blaster turrets and old-fashioned landmines around the perimeter burned down or blew up their scouts, and a brigade of Monitors waddled out of the bunkers to man anti-personnel weapons.

The Captain placed a call for air support, but nobody onboard the *Barracuda* picked up. Fucking slackers. No matter...

Something fell at her feet. The shock collar. She looked up

at Poly. The Warpie rebel wore her human form with a primitive bikini made of laser-tanned Monitor hide and a lizard skull for a helmet, but something more subtly far-reaching was different. Was she taller, more muscular, or was something missing?

"Have I redeemed myself yet?" Lilith whined and pranced around Poly's feet, grinding herself against her legs and pleading for her to change back into a dog and play.

Callista lit a long black cigarette. "Oh sure, you've done a great job digging us deeper into the mess you created, but we should be back in the black soon, and you've given me what I need. So, full marks. You're promoted back to two legs."

It was the look in her eye. That *woo-woo* lovestruck look was finally gone, and good fucking riddance. Callista sighed with relief, though this might complicate matters.

"What do you mean? What did I give you?"

Tossing her bangs, she flipped a shoulder at the anarchic army of dogs licking their crotches. "Shock troops. If they'll follow you to freedom, they'll follow you anywhere, right?"

"Where are we going?"

"To save my species' homeworld, which totally doesn't deserve it, but if the rest of the universe hates us that much, it's worth doing."

"But my people are simple, peace-loving creatures."

"If they're so great, why'd you leave?"

"It was my only hope to find someone strong enough to set them free. I thought, even if you could not love, at least you were moved to pity…"

"Pity?" Callista laughed until she coughed. "We're humans, baby. We save our pity for ourselves. Our brains are so fucked up, they're a controlled substance. The universe is better off without us. The only one more fucked-up than us is you, for trusting us. Now, be a love and go lead that suicide charge."

Poly hissed through her teeth, but she changed back into a dog. While el Magico boiled a pheromone potion in a tiny cauldron and blew its scarlet vapor over the army, Callista climbed up onto a cargo container and dangled her leash, which immediately got the dogs' attention.

"I'm not much for inspirational speeches, so... Who wants to go walkies?"

Callista turned and flung the leash over the electrified fence. The army of Warpie dogs took off after it, leaping and being electrocuted until they shorted out the barrier. The surviving dogs ran over the smoldering bodies to leap onto the tarmac of the compound. Monitors caught them in a crossfire, but before long, they were coming over the fence on all sides and bounding headlong into the gun emplacements, their concerted barking gradually crowding out the dwindling rasp of plasma blasters, until there was only the dogs.

Callista, Lilith and el Magico climbed the dogpile and crossed over the fence, strolled through a minefield of copulating dogs to the central bunker. El Magico hacked the door defenses and Callista strode in with Poly at her heels.

"It shouldn't be you," Poly pleaded. "If you overthrow them, you'll only be another Stone Face conqueror... My people must see one of their own take the throne, or they'll never know freedom!"

"But that's what I am, darling," Callista said. "A Stone Face conqueror, that's me." Pointing at the stubby heated basking rock behind which skulked the Monitor Viceroy of Warpworld. "The last thing you want to do is set these idiots free. I've seen freedom. It's more toxic than Coca Cola. And as for your people..."

With her blowtorch, Callista herded the viceroy into a corner of the bunker, then skillfully seared his Warpie garments until they surrendered and left the cowering four-eyed lizard naked and pleading for his life.

"See, I may not be an experienced freedom-fighter, but these assholes had such shitshow defenses, you have to wonder why."

Closing in, she pressed the nozzle of the flamethrower into the tender spot between the viceroy's four crossed eyes. "Show us," she said.

The viceroy closed his eyes and melted.

Out of the foam of liquefied scales emerged a glittering, googly-eyed bowel-blob, which prostrated itself before the Captain.

"Your 'people' successfully infiltrated their conquerors a long time ago, in a silent, if not bloodless coup, and then just replaced them…"

"No!" Poly cried out.

"And carried on oppressing their former friends and loved ones. Maybe they were even worse than the real lizards, because they hated themselves almost as much as they came to hate you."

The miserable Warpie viceroy pressed itself against the nozzle of the flamethrower, begging for execution. "Suffer, baby," Callista said, and put out her cigarette on its head.

"So what happens now? Surely you can't think to take my people with you on your insane campaign to save your dead race?"

Callista stopped and looked her up and down with fresh annoyance. "Who died and made you the plot-police?" Lighting another cigarette off her flamethrower, she said, "You're right. It'd be selfish of me to save these people just to feed them to a meat-grinder. Besides, they deserve to be free."

Strolling back outside, they found the Warpie dog army watching them with eerie attentiveness, as if they were eating the last piece of fried chicken on the planet.

Looking around at her feet, Callista picked up a severed Monitor head and held it aloft, which set the dogs howling. "We have killed your leaders! You are now free! Free to be and do whatever you want! Welcome to total freedom, fuckers!"

El Magico flung out two fistfuls of purple smoke and set off a whooping siren that dissolved into sick dubstep beats. The dogs howled and stopped being dogs.

All across the compound, each and every Warpie was set free of its traumatic enslavement. Drunk on freedom and whatever it'd just inhaled, each tapped into its own heart's desire and turned itself inside out. For one precious, fleeting moment, it looked like an intergalactic zoo, a freaky alien United Nations. Then natural predators spotted natural prey, and the collective dissolved into a riot of shapeshifting, eating, killing amid some very poignant yet doomed cuddling.

Poly screamed and became as big and loud as she could, but she was just one more Warpie screaming among thousands.

"Let it go, kid," Callista said in her ear, pulling her not ungently towards the rows of blastboat launchers behind the bunker. "You don't belong here with them. You knew that when you left. They'll figure it out or they won't. Safe money says a few of them will adopt Monitor shapes and everything'll be back where it was tomorrow. You can't do anything for them, there's no point in trying. Come on… be a pirate."

Poly resisted, looking over her shoulder one last time. Then she shoved the Captain to her knees.

"Who d'you think you're pushing, bitch…" Callista turned to snap Poly's neck just as a predictable last lone Monitor popped up from behind the launchers and fired a plasma blaster at her. "Endothermic whore!" it screamed as it shot. "Viviparous bitch!"

Callista returned fire and burned the ugly lizard's head down to a glass stump before she realized Poly was gone, and where she was.

The Warpie had wrapped herself around the Captain like a bulletproof vest and absorbed what she could not deflect of the deadly plasma beams. Now she fell away from Callista's patent leather curves in sizzling, molten chunks.

Callista fell to her knees and scooped up as much of Poly as she could before el Magico dragged her by her collar to an idling blastboat in front of a lunging, wailing wall of Warpie dogs, Monitors and Monitor-dogs.

Her hands clutched a single solid object that might contain enough intact genetic material to regenerate her, but to her disgust, when she wiped away the slime, she found it was only a belt buckle.

I STAYED ON FOR 1.5 DAYS!

15

The blastboat was snatched out of its corkscrew trajectory by the *Barracuda*, which lay in geostationary orbit amid the wreckage of the Monitor flying fortress.

Captain Callista Chrome strode through the airlock before it irised open, trying to reach Skink on the intra-ship channel, and walked into a golden crook that cracked her bubble helmet in half.

"What the fuck?" She staggered, dropping what she'd salvaged of Poly.

Tutankhaten stood over her, holding the crook and a big golden thermos with an ibis head for a stopper. Flanked by a pair of jackal-headed cargo loader bots, the pharaoh cackled as he unveiled his nefarious plan. It might've been impressive, if her translator didn't interpret his ravings in a piping helium falsetto.

"Who mocks the grand design of the gods? Dear lady, you are the reincarnation of my predestined wife, empress Nefertiti IX, whom I shall restore to glory before impregnating with the spawn of Aten. Search your heart, you know it to be true!"

Rubbing her forehead, Callista said, "I think I'd remember that…"

Brandishing the canopic jar, Tutankhaten replied, "You will remember all, when your true heart is restored to your sadly desecrated earthly vessel." Turning to the cargo bots, he shouted, "Guards! Bathe her and bring her to my tomb!"

"You know," Callista said, "normally... this would be exactly the kind of game I'd go for, but I'm really not in the mood right now... and you made me drop her!" She punched the pharaoh in the junk, then set him on fire. She caught the canopic jar as he dropped it, dumped the shriveled gray pickle of Nefertiti IX's heart out on the deck and dropped the half-melted remains of her Warpie concubine into it.

While the cargo robots sprayed the pharaoh down with fire extinguishers, she stomped up to the bridge, arriving just as Skink skidded into view wearing only a pair of boxers, which were on backwards.

Saluting, Skink gushed, "Sorry, your worship, I was, erm... just performing routine maintenance, you know how you're always on us about the ducts, like, and... thought I'd make it a surprise..." Finally, he noticed her eye welling up with tears. "Uh... Callista... If you want to talk..."

With an inarticulate shriek of unhinged rage, Callista flung the canopic jar at Skink and stormed off to her cabin with Lilith hot on her heels.

Skink caught the jar in the gut, toppled over into the bulkhead, grunted, "Where to next, Captain?"

Callista slammed her hatch without reply. El Magico knelt before the warp drive incubator, pouring out a circle of white powder around it and himself, and with gusts of smoke from his mumbling lips, set about confusing the computer.

"What the fuck are you looking at? Are *you* judging me, too?" Callista screamed at Lilith, who guiltily averted her eyes and strove to get the last gobs of peanut butter off the roof of her mouth.

Who did that little bitch think she was?

Callista Chrome was already a legend in a field where few aspiring pirates survived their first deep space raid. But she had no illusions about why her crew followed her. In spite of her audacity, brilliance and ruthless efficiency, they all nursed a big wet one for her, and hoped she'd come around someday.

"Only love and death can make us become better than we are," she mewled in a sneering approximation of Poly's voice. Love! Strangers always thought you owed them something in return for their love.

Maybe Callista had felt something for the Warpie, but nothing like love. She showed the doomed little waif what happens when you try to help, what ordinary people do with total freedom... but what did she hope to get out of it? To crush her spirit, to make her more malleable, or to awaken something inside her worthy of more than pity?

Well, it didn't matter now, because in the end, Poly had played true to her doormat nature, sacrificing herself unnecessarily...

But was she really just succumbing to instinct, or was it that other, more troublesome thing? Maybe Poly had thrown herself into the path of the plasma beams to flip the script on her, giving up her life like a beesting, tearing out her guts just to ruin the Captain's day, to prove that nothing in her life was as powerful or as worth having as something she could not allow herself to feel.

And her day was ruined, wasn't it? *Admit it,* she told herself. *You miss that freak like the Devil misses angel food cake.*

The little bitch was gone, but she needn't get the last word. Callista would show her that one could make a grand, heroic, self-sacrificing gesture without love coming into the equation.

Callista took to the stars like a duck to duck soup because it offered her an arena to turn loose her uncontrollable id, to wreak havoc with impunity upon an endless procession of self-centered shithead aliens. She never set out to save anyone, least of all herself. But somehow, she found herself the lone champion of the rotten species that sent her screaming into space tearing her hair out, in the first fucking place.

Hell, she'd save the whole fucking Earth just to prove she could, and then blow it up herself.

Callista toweled herself off and threw the empty Skippy Super Smooth jar into the recycler. Spraying her naked body with a coat of defensive chrome polymer, she wrapped herself in a cape of nebula-moth scales trimmed with the same remarkable—and, thanks to Callista's designer, extinct—lifeform's feathery antennae, she leapt out of bed and swept over to the communicator.

"Skink, set a course for—"

"Warworld III off the starboard bow, Captain," Skink cut in.

"About damn time," she said, and hung up.

As already established somewhere above, Warworld III is something of a noteworthy shithole. In fact, *Xloviovryx's Compleat Intergalactic Guide To Shitholes* rates it three stars, recommending it only for tourists seeking a truly momentous assisted suicide.

Alien slavers had been dumping intractable abductees on Warworld III for centuries. After Warworld I and Warworld II used fission bomb propulsion to turn their entire planets into roving dreadnaughts of death and, perhaps inevitably, crashed into each other, the entire system of Warworld III was under interdiction and patrol by unmanned drones, but there was little chance of anyone on the planet achieving interstellar flight before one of their adversaries kicked them over.

Ruled by a volatile patchwork of tribal alliances including the Space Aztecs, Space Vikings and the lost Roanoke colony, Warworld III existed in a constant state of internecine warfare for all of its five thousand-odd years of largely unrecorded history.

Until last month.

***

Looking down on it from the howdah strapped to the back of a war-mastodon parading down the renamed Avenue of the Children Flowers, she had to admit they seemed serious about this peace thing, even if the streets were still paved with skulls.

Construction crews everywhere tore down the siege engines, defensive fortifications, atrocity monuments and forests of skeletons on pikes to replace them with strip malls, condo complexes, convenience stores, massage parlors. Lines of men with prosthetic legs, arms and faces waited outside a shiny new factory. It reminded her of the worst place in the universe. It reminded her of home.

"It is not much," Bludbeard rumbled over her shoulder, "but a humble beginning." Chieftain of the Berserker clan of the Space Viking Nation, Bludbeard Ironwaffelsen was harder to look at than the half-assed recovery efforts.

According to legend, Thorwald Ironwaffelsen was moved to seek an unprecedented peace treaty with his clan's mortal enemies, the Judge Crater Gang, by his only begotten daughter. In defiance of all he knew, the chieftain went unarmed into the Crater Gang's stronghold, only to emerge with his entire face flayed away down to the chin and dangling from his jawline like a gory beard, driving his beloved daughter Wiglaf to flee her troubled homeworld in shame.

She looked over a crowd gathered round a street musician, a horribly scarred young man who had plugged a bastard sword into a tower of amplifiers and was reverently stroking it to elicit a throbbing, doomful Theramin drone that made her fillings rise up from her cavities and demand blood and souls.

"You've done a lot in a month," Callista said, hoping it sounded less idiotic than it sounded to the big idiot.

"We have had no guidance from beyond our skies," Bludbeard admitted, "but now you have come from the motherworld to bless our cease-fire with your great gift, I dare to hope that the fragile peace will hold, and we can join the brotherhood of humanity in the stars. I only wish my beloved daughter Wiglaf could see it..."

Callista nodded solemnly as the mastodon shuffled past yet another mile-long unemployment line. She bit her tongue before it could tell him that Wiglaf hadn't run away to find peace, but refuge from idiotic, bloody-minded men.

Her gloved hands tightly interlaced round the black glass bowling bag which the chieftain had somehow decided was some kind of peace offering brought by Callista Chrome as an emissary from the federation of humanity. She wasn't looking forward to disabusing him of all his naïve misconceptions, any more than she was about coming clean about what was in the bowling bag.

Best to get the easy stuff out of the way, first.

She turned and leaned back on the railing, letting her cloak fall open and presenting herself to best effect. "Well Chief, it's funny you should mention the good old brotherhood, because right now, we were really hoping for less of that peace business, and more of the, um, other? You see, we're in kind of a bind with the Intergalactic Narcotic Enforcement Force, and they're going to blow up the Earth, which would be a huge blow to that whole peace thing. Honestly, if you want to cement a peaceful alliance, there's no better way than to link arms and go kick the shit out of somebody else together."

Bludbeard shook his head sadly, though his eyes practically left a snail-trail down her cleavage. With broad stretches of tundra for shoulders, rippling, battle-scarred arms and massive, skull-crushing hands, he was far from undesirable, if only he'd stitch his face back onto his head, or at least moisturize the taut straps of exposed muscle twanging away on his skull. "We have heard all this before from soft tongues who would use our valor for their own gross ends. We have beaten our swords into... the opposite of swords. This is now our way. To go back would mean only bloodshed and chaos come again."

"But your honorable tradition of forever war was the only thing that kept the aliens away from your door. Once word gets out that you've gone soft…"

"Soft, eh?" Bludbeard stomped his foot so heard the mastodon collapsed with a burst kidney. "Woman, I'll have you know that my own daughter…"

Callista unzipped the bowling bag and let it fall away. "This one?"

All the color went out of Bludbeard's dangling face. "Wiglaf!"

The wide, blue-steel eyes of Wiglaf Bludbeardsdottir stared out through the coating of frost on the Perspex cylinder. "You might not give a shit about the Earth, but the alien assholes who cut off your daughter's head give a shit about you. Human brains are the new drug of choice, darling."

"She is… Is she…?"

Callista pointed out the dimly blinking light on the to bottom of the cylinder. "Not yet, but time's a-wasting. I know peace is a nice idea, but payback is a bitch, and she's hungry."

Cradling the frosty cylinder in his massive hands, Bludbeard took silent counsel with his gods. Finally, he said, "All shall be settled by the old ways, which are best."

Callista purred, "I like the sound of that."

"You shall face a champion in trial by combat. If you prevail, then we will follow you to war."

Just for kicks, she asked, "And if I lose?"

"Then my daughter will walk again with a new body…" Looking up from the icy face of his only begotten daughter, he made a single word into a nail of hoarfrost that he drove through her forehead.

"Yours."

16

"Let it be known forevermore," cried the skald of Bludbeard Ironwaffeldottir, "that on this day was decided the fate of the peace-loving peoples of Warworld III, in a trial by combat between our champion..."

The skald trailed off as he tried to read the vellum scroll in his trembling hands. Like all poets and literate types of his clan, the skald had both eyes put out at an early age, and a pair of raven chicks stuffed into the sockets. Now, the cawing, claustrophobic carrion birds competed with the skald's quavering voice for the attention of the unruly mob of space vikings in the great hall of the Berserker clan, but somehow, they enabled him to read the words, when they felt like it.

Putting a pair of tiny spectacles on the beak of each raven, the skald squinted, "As our champion... Grim Skallagrimsen, bearer of the wolf-banner!"

An iron-thewed warrior with a wolf's head for a hat rose up out of the masses, flexing his oiled muscles and brandishing a three-bladed vorpal sword. With a pantherish flourish, he sprang over the rail and down into the arena pit, still stained and stinking from the dogs, bears and stranger combatants that had suffered for these imbeciles' inability to reinvent television.

"And in the unlikely event of his fall… his second… Sigurd Fnordbane, bearer of the bear-standard!" An even bigger, bulkier man, wearing only, yes, a cave bear's head and pelt, stood up to menace the crowd and spill his neighbors' ale before settling back onto his well-worn bench.

Almost as an afterthought, the skald added, "And challenging them, an interloper who would see the united peace-loving people of Warworld III go to war in the boundless deeps of space and shed their blood for a foreign world that never knew our faces…" Primed by this lickspittle diatribe, the crowd booed like any union hall full of blue-collar wrestling fanatics. "Captain… Clitoris… Crom…"

Fucking idiots.

Clad in a loincloth and battle-bra of cheap silver chainmail sure to turn her tits green if she broke a sweat, Callista dropped into the arena opposite the wolf-headed warrior and tossed an empty ale flagon over her shoulder. Anything to get the burnt dirt taste of el Magico's dexterity potion out of her throat.

Watching him limber up, his sculpted torso twisting and narrow hips thrusting, gnarly arms whipping the sword in a deadly cyclone above his head, she got kind of hot, until she remembered that she was here to kill him.

Then she got wet.

"Go easy on me, hon," she said. "I'm just a girl…"

Circling Grim Skallagrimsen, she absently twirled her sword, eyes pinned to the creamy marmoreal density of his clenched buttocks, the scrumptious play of light on the bricks of his abdomen, the impressive bulge of his loincloth. Though she couldn't see his face for all the wolf bullshit, his hesitant posture told her he was embarrassed to be fighting a woman.

The mob roared with scorn and frustration, as if their champion was forced to wear a dress. Maybe they figured a woman wouldn't put on much of a show, or maybe they wanted to see a woman die more than they wanted to go do what they lived for. Even the shield-maidens, in their dank corner of the hall, shrieked for her to be swiftly beheaded.

Men.

Did they really expect her to piss her silver panties at this steak-headed display? She would show them there was more than one way to kill a man, and get her rocks off in the bargain.

Forcing contact, Callista abruptly reversed her orbit and raised her sword, but just as her opponent braced and threw up his blade to block her, she pivoted and executed a fast, nasty move that let him see the lithe fluidity of her form and the blinding quickness of her reflexes. Rolling her hips and throwing out her chest so her breasts popped out of the useless battle-bra, she immediately saw results in his jerky recovery.

"Come on," she cooed, tossing the bra into the audience, "let's make this interesting." God damn, she forgot how horny the dexterity tonic made her.

Now, he had more urgent things on his mind than cutting off her head. Which made him angry. Which made him lash out clumsily with his sword, trying to take her head in one stroke. She easily ducked under the whirring trio of steel and knelt before Grim's pelvis, and with a deft hand, caressed his bulge. It squirmed under her fingers like an angry snake, diverting blood from his furiously working muscles, diverted concentration from his brain.

Before he could arrest the wild swing, she'd cut off his breechclout and sidled back out of reach.

The crowd laughed so hard that the naked warrior roared back and swung his sword as if to cut out all their tongues. She came up behind him and swiftly squeezed his ass, then drove a thumb up his rectum.

Grim Skallagrimsen leapt into the air and landed facing her. The hardboiled eggs of his eyes gleamed at her out from under the fanged muzzle of the wolf on his head.

"This is boring," Callista said, "you're boring everybody." Pulling the chain on her loincloth, she stepped out of it to the scandalized howls of the crowd. "Maybe you should call your friend in here to come help."

It took guts not to run for your life in the other direction, but it was all Callista could do not to laugh. In the midst of all that indomitable muscle, the bobbing, flopping uncircumcised peg of his fully erect dong completely deflated any sense of threat she should've felt.

But he kept trying to cut her head off, bless his heart. She crossed swords with him too many times to count, her speed making a joke of his strength, parrying his attacks without letting her blade get trapped between his. Finally, when he looked ready, she let him have her sword, riding it down to the hilt so they came close enough to kiss.

She darted in and shoved her tongue into his mouth, shocking him so he choked on his own spit. She fell back so quickly he overbalanced, then kicked his left knee just as it compressed with his full weight.

Screaming, Grim Skallagrimsen tripped and fell, rolling away towards the arena wall. Callista stepped on his knee again, making him scream and pinning him supine on the ground before her. She straddled him and dropped onto his magnificent cock.

The whole length of it slammed into her like a subway train, punching her cervix just exactly right. The shock of warmth that turned her guts to molten gold. The warrior's screams turned to gasping whoops. Trapping him between her thighs and clasping him tightly with her pelvic muscles, she pinned his hands above his head.

"Give, give, give," she panted, pinching and twisting her nipples, arching her back, "Take, take, take." She was so close, almost over the edge—

Spasming and drumming the flagstones with his heels, Grim Skallagrimsen came inside her, thrashing beneath her like a lion as every jaw in the hall dropped open in abject outrage. All except for about half of the shield-maidens, who cried out her name and blew her kisses.

Winking at them, she looked down on her would-be murderer and slapped him full across the face. "Is that *it*? Did I tell you could come?" She slapped him again, knocking the wolf-head away from his face. She almost felt bad, he was kind of cute. "I'm barely warmed up, you little worm."

Lifting herself off him, she let the pearly droplets of his premature semen drip out of her to pool on his chest and called out, "Next!"

Rising like a mushroom cloud from his bench, Sigurd Fnordbane took up a double-headed battle-axe and sprang over the rail, landed running towards Callista with his axe held high.

The Captain only had enough time to pick up her sword, dig a bit of gravel out from under a fingernail and execute another shit-hot dance move before Sigurd arrived.

She raised her sword and stepped back to telegraph another ambush. Sigurd turned on one clawed boot to split her down the middle. She leapt inside the swing, drove the heel of her hand into his sternum, then his nose, and climbed the hulking berserker like a tree.

Choking on his inhaled blood, wracked by a seizure that forced his tongue out between his clenched teeth, Sigurd sat down hard, then fell on his back with Callista clutching his head in the vice of her thighs, trapping his face in her sopping vagina.

She held the sword poised over his eyes so whatever part of him still kept his heart beating and lungs pumping realized it'd be a very bad idea to bite her. "That's right… clean it all up… your friend made quite a mess, didn't he?"

Maybe it was his death-spasm that did the trick, but it was worth it. Fnordbane's tongue went rigid, yet vibrating long after all brain function had ceased. Callista came and came, gyrating and grinding her cunt into the berserker's face. The unbridled animus of the crowd only lifted her higher, their rage setting her free of hers. For a moment, she knew total contentment.

But then, as almost always, a guy ruined it.

Grim Skallagrimsen had recovered his sword, and the refractory period on this planet was something else, there had to be something in the water. Little Grim wagged at her as he came running, but she wasn't in the mood, anymore.

Callista flung her sword like a lawn dart and with the same languid precision of those bygone outdoor toys of a simpler, more deadly yesteryear, it seemed to float before the wolf-warrior just before it slid home in his left eyesocket.

At last, the crowd fell silent.

Callista got up off the cooling but still functionally rigid tongue of Sigurd Fnordbane and strutted over to the other corpse, rolling her hips and stretching so that even the cheap seats could see the fluids of their dead champions streaming down her inner thigh.

Pulling the sword free, she looked round the hall and shouted, "You people are adorable. You think you're special, because you like war? Humans who like war? Big fucking deal, you might as well name your planet Cheesecake Factory.

"Every other intelligent lifeform in the universe despises us and calls us a cancer. They think they're better off without us. Are they?"

"Probably…" someone replied, amid a rumble of confused murmuring. She was getting too sophisticated for them. Too bad.

"And do you know why they hate us? It's not because we like war. Everybody loves war. If you were any other species, you'd probably be in charge of everything. And it's not because we lie… although truth be told, we are the best in the galaxy at it.

"No, they hate us because we *dream*.

"We can dream of a better way of life while up to our necks in shit, and that's why they hate us.

"We can see ourselves as heroes when they're pissing down our necks, and that's why they hate us.

"We can keep a place in our hearts for things that can't

and should never be, and love them, and somehow that drives them crazy. They say it's because we're insane. But I think it drives them insane that they can't do what we do, so while they burn our worlds out of the sky with one hand, they try on our clothes, our culture, our dreams with the other.

"So, I ask you... Are we weeds, or roses? Are we just rats in the walls of this shitty galaxy, or are we warriors, lovers, artists and dreamers who'll fuck up anyone who tries to stop us?

"Well, what are we?"

Silence was her only answer.

But then, from off across the arena, there came a single, slow, sarcastic pair of clapping hands.

"Bravo! An inspiring performance! And a most stirring speech, even if it was a bit over their heads."

Callista raised her sword. Fucking Interlocutor! She looked around the hall and saw the same vacant expression gawping at her, the same half-lidded eyes, the same gossamer runners of drool from every paralyzed, gaping mouth. "What did you do to them?"

The Interlocutor strolled up in a freshly printed replica of its earwig-silverfish body, but she quickly noticed a host of subtle modifications. Maybe it was because it used the same printers that manufactured Warworld III's ubiquitous prosthetic limbs, but its exoskeleton bulged with phony muscles, and between its hind legs wagged a reasonable facsimile of a semi-erect penis. Sure, it enticed her the same way a pair of truck balls hanging off the trailer hitch of a Chevy pickup with A WOMAN'S PLACE IS ON MY FACE and FUCK JANE FONDA all over the bumper, but she couldn't take her eyes off it, just the same, even as it stirred and expanded under her attention.

The Interlocutor cleared its synthetic throat. "My eyes are up here, Captain. I only gave them peace. Who do you think it was that brokered this treaty? These insane but simple organisms lack the imagination to picture a cat if you describe it, let alone dream of a better world. Aphantasia, I believe the clinical term for it is. Generations of fighting constant war weed out those with imagination quite quickly, for they are often cowards or crazy, owing to their unfortunate neurology.

"But you were never going to win them over. Because they're already ours.

"Those shiny new factories outside are harvesting their brains. Low-grade product, to be sure, owing to malnutrition and propaganda, but it's a seller's market. And that's all I'm trying to get out of you, Callista. I want you for a partner. Just show us where the rest of the human worlds are, and the secret of the quantum uncertainty engine. The worst thing that could happen to you if you cooperate is you'll become the wealthiest human in the galaxy. That's all you want, right? After all, you've been selling them for years. Why the crisis of conscience now?"

Somewhere during this monologue, Callista jabbed the tip of her tongue into one of her molars, summoning Skink. Just as the Interlocutor reached out a forelimb to offer her a cigarette injection, the dropship came smashing through the roof of the mead-hall and squashed the Interlocutor into the stones.

"What took you so fucking long?" Callista grated as the hatch irised open, but rather than climb aboard, she ran to the rail, climbed up into the chieftain's box and claimed the frosty cylinder propped up on the arm of Bludbeard's throne. The bastard was using it to chill his ale.

"You don't deserve her," she said, tucking the cylinder under her arm and dumping the ale in the paralyzed chieftain's lap.

17

"Skink!"

Callista Chrome strode onto the bridge of her ship looking for someone to throw Wiglaf's head at, when she saw a statuesque naked female form sitting backwards on the first mate's chair. Skink's bandy blue legs protruded out from underneath the rhythmically clenching and releasing buttocks of Wiglaf's body, which had no head. A cluster of tubes and wires trailed away from the neatly cauterized neck-stump.

"Skink!" Callista's scream trailed off in a confused, breathless question. "Is that what I think it is?"

"Right of salvage!" Skink screamed, struggling to shut off the copulating corpse.

Callista cracked a rare, exhausted smile. "I love you so hard right now."

Skink squinted, sensing but not quite seeing a trap. "Really? You, erm... wanna get in on this?"

Callista cracked the icy cylinder and dropped Wiglaf's head in his lap. He screamed when the burning cold flesh of her face touched his belly, but couldn't get out from under her body. "Fix her and wake up Magico. And bring me a triple espresso, a pack of smokes and a shot of adrenochrome so I can get us the fuck out of here."

Finally, Skink reached the remote controlling Wiglaf's body. Ordering it to take its head to sickbay, he stood up and pulled on his boxers. "Did you get the barbarian army you wanted, then?"

The Captain strutted to her chair and reclined in it, strapping on her pilot's gloves and a VR helmet, jacked into the sockets behind her ears. "No, and we don't need them."

"So where we going?"

"Earth. We're going to save it. That ought to show the little bastards…"

"That would be impressive… But Cap'n… the Earth is, like, gone…"

"Sure, now, but seven months ago…"

Magico came shambling in rubbing his black faceted eyes and began loading a dose of unnervingly bright glowing powder into a slender bamboo straw half again his own height.

Skink blinked. "I don't get it."

"And you never will," Callista replied. Punching buttons on her console, she assumed direct control of the ship and flexed her arms, reveling in sharing the *Barracuda*'s five-armed, radial symmetry. "Did it ever occur to you that a ship capable of instantaneous travel is essentially a time machine?"

"Er… no…"

"And if said travel is accomplished by confusing the warp drive as to its location in space-time, then it's a relatively simple matter to travel backwards through time by just lying to it…"

"Wow, so the ship is a time machine?"

"Try to keep up, little man."

"But the whole premise shits on the chest of all known science—"

"Fuck science," she snarled. "Science is for people who can't handle drugs."

"But if we go back and stop the whole Narc armada, won't they just come back the next day and do it again, so we'll have to go back and fix it again… you see where this is headed?"

"Not if we make them sorry they ever heard of us…"

"Pretty sure they already are, milady."

Callista lifted the helmet and fixed Skink with a baleful, warning stare. Her hand absently reached down and snatched up a black leather riding crop. "Are you disobeying an order? A *direct* order?"

"Not a bit of it, your worship. It's just… you're going to throw our lives away to save seven billion dead assholes that you hate to push back on the guilt you feel for pushing away someone who truly loved you."

"In a word… yes. What's your problem?"

"Just trying to keep your motivations straight, love." Looking at a blinking idiot light on his board, Skink added, "I've got seven Mercantile dropships spinning up from Warworld III on an intercept course, Mum…"

"Good. Magico?"

The alien shaman put the business end of the bamboo shaft against the intake on the warp drive incubator and chanted a susurrant mantra into it while Callista counted down. When she said, "One," he took a deep breath, and when she said, "Zero," he blew the drug into the unborn baby's brain.

The universe went sideways. Then it went backwards, then it swirled around them like the flush of a toilet, dropping them into an interstitial zone where a parsec is both a unit of time and distance.

18

She dropped the can.

Her legs spasmed and kicked out at the pedals of the car—the car?

She rubbed her eyes. Looked around, taking it in like another trip. Good one, she thought. I was... She tried to recover the recursive chemical dreams before they receded into her memory hole, but clawing them back was like picking up pages written on wet toilet paper, she was left with handfuls of squishy mush.

"Barracuda" faded out on the classic rock station on her shitty pullout stereo, and "Barbarella" by The Bongos came on.

I was a warrior queen, she thought... *no, I was a diabolical concubine... no, I was a...* She giggled to herself, it was so pointless trying to remember them all, when they were gone so quick, but she could always take another hit and do it all again.

She reached down between her legs and fumbled around the floorboards. Empty cigarette packs, bottlecaps, condom wrappers, scratched CD's, strip club flyers, *there*. Her cracked fingernails tickled the icy surface of the cylinder. After several clumsy attempts, she got the can back.

Oh Dust-Buster, you're my boon companion, keeper of my secrets. She must be pretty bad off, if she was down to huffing the shit you use to blow dandruff and potato chip crumbs out of your computer keyboard, alone in her car. The heady mix of nitrous oxide and chlorodifluoromethane stirred up her brains with a stick. But no street drugs you could find around here could give you the kind of incredibly vivid yet elusive sense of whole other lives folded into a momentary seizure. Those other lives glittered and faded out now with a melancholy sense of having been more real than wherever and whatever she was.

And where the hell, what the hell was she?

She was in the parking lot of the Anchorage Holiday Inn, her fifteen year old Isuzu Rodeo slewed across two spots under a marquee sign that said WELCOME PALMER 10TH HIGH SCHOOL REUNION! LET'S MAKE SOME MEMORIES!

Jesus fuck me gently, that can't be right.

She was wearing a faded t-shirt from Little Bitches Kozy Kennel Gentleman's Club in Anchorage, torn sweatpants and mismatched flats. She was thirty pounds overweight and her scary-large breasts ached when she probed them, but at least they were real.

She looked in her purse, but couldn't find an invitation, naturally… Who would they have to talk shit about, if she was standing next to them? She couldn't find her phone, but here was a wallet telling her she was named Karen Cole, and she lived in an apartment in Wasilla. Also a pepper-spray canister and a .32 automatic with a loaded clip.

What the fuck am I doing here? The things that just happened… that life… Did I make it all up?

She looked in the mirror and gasped. She had two eyes. Of course she did, why wouldn't she? She looked down at herself, held her hand up in front of her face and tripped out on it. Whoa, depth perception.

Then she looked down.

Jesus, she was fat. Even her fingers were plump. No wonder the club fired her, no wonder her webcam was pulling in fewer than fourteen daily hits, all nonpaying, all angry ex's.

Fat, flat broke and fucked in the head. She rolled the can in her hand. Dust-Buster? Jesus, couldn't she even steal nitrous tanks from a dentist's office, like normal people?

Who am I? What the fuck happened to me? What was I going to do with my life, before it happened?

For just a moment, she had a sort of flashback—just a fragment of that beautiful memory, of being somebody feared, legendary, even. Aliens in far-flung backwater cantinas talked shit about her in awed whispers halfway across the galaxy. The name of her cunt was a curse in more than one xenomorph language.

Her nipples stiffened, her G-string slick with girl-juice. *I was somebody…*

Then it was gone, like any daydream that passed through her brain while she worked the pole, trying not to see the awful thoughts spilling out the empty eyes of the pukes in the front row, the dollar pushers, the ones trying to look safe and real, as if every dollar they made her crawl for was an installment on her purchase.

She hefted the gun and it passed through her mind that this was just a simulation, that the barely-remembered dream was the reality, this was a trap, and she could go back anytime she wanted. All she had to do was stick the gun in her mouth and pull the trigger.

Was that why she was here? That sounded like something she'd do, or daydream about doing… Go up on stage, take a bow in front of her fellow alumni, say, "Thanks for ruining my life," and blow her brains out.

Then she lifted her purse, which was too small to fit the extra box of ammunition resting under it, and she remembered why she was here. Lighting a cigarette, she looked in the mirror and told herself, *Let's make some memories!*

After digging around in the Hefty bag of work outfits in her trunk, she found a pair of matching(!) heels and a cocktail dress with only a few cigarette burns in it. She thought about changing in the backseat, but noticed the overflowing grocery bags, boxes of old paperbacks infested with earwigs and silverfish and piles of shit pressing against the windows and wondered if she still lived in that apartment in Wasilla.

She stumbled a bit as she strolled through the lobby of the Holiday Inn. The front desk people looked at her, but didn't immediately pick up phones when she veered into the restroom, bless their hearts.

Changing in the toilet stall was an experience. Someone, probably from the front desk, came in and ostentatiously cleared her throat a few times to let anyone inside know they probably shouldn't smoke or snort anything in here, but at least the bitch wasn't waiting when she came out.

Back out in the lobby, she scanned the desk until she caught the smoky eye of the bowl haircut brunette who'd taken it upon herself to monitor her activities. Nametag said BONNIE. She went over and asked Bonnie where the Palmer High reunion was.

Looking mildly relieved, Bonnie pointed down past the elevators, where a big free-standing placard repeated the horseshit on the marquee outside.

Karen thanked her, stuck the nozzle of the Dust-Buster can in her mouth and took a big hit, blowing out her cheeks and bugging her eyes, hissed it out as she staggered through neon fog towards the double doors and the poorly-amplified dance mix of her high school prom.

The duster didn't take her away, but it put a nice spin on the room, let her feel the winds of causality lifting her through the doorway. Adopting the frigid poise of a dowager empress, she nodded regally to the chubby bowl-cut former ASB secretary guarding the door—another Bonnie, if memory served—who nervously scanned the unclaimed nametags on the registration table.

Only about a dozen fugitive names lay under her obsessively manicured nails, and none of them were hers. There were three hundred twenty-two seniors in her graduating class, and she'd immediately forgotten ninety percent of them the day after prom.

Prom—oh God, it was at this hotel, in this very room, wasn't it? After they held the homecoming dance in Palmer's half-abandoned shopping mall and a bunch of "bad and almost certainly drunk kids" (including, if not led by, herself) broke into and vandalized the K-Mart, the school was shamed into springing for a hotel in the nearest big town.

They hadn't even changed the ugly burnt umber-maroon-sienna-avocado-goldenrod carpet, but it was still doing a hell of a job hiding her indelible puke stains, ten years later.

Everybody was staring at her as she picked up a random nametag and scribbled her name on it in Sharpie and pinned it on her dress. The pin tore the flimsy fabric and pricked one of her infuriatingly bloated breasts. She took it off and looked at it. She'd written CALLISTA CHROME. Why the fuck had she written her stage name? Well, why the fuck not?

She pinned the nametag on, nodded to a nervous couple scooting towards the door, and made a similarly urgent trip across the ballroom to the bar.

"Gimme vodka… not the cup, gimme the bottle…"

The bartender stared at her, then over her shoulder. He was the only black guy in the place. He looked so familiar…

"Do I know you?" she asked. "You remind me of somebody, but he's not black, he's blue…"

He heaved a disgusted sigh and put the bottle on the counter, turned away.

"Karen! So glad you could make it! We hadn't heard from you in so long, nobody expected you… We thought you'd dropped off the face of the Earth."

"You wish." Taking a long, incendiary pull off the bottle, she turned to look at her oldest, best friend in the world. "You should've asked your husband… He's a regular at Little Bitches."

Mindy laughed too hard, took the vodka from her hand and downed a third of it. "OK, listen, Karen. We were besties a long time, but you went way off the map. This is a night for celebrating happy memories, and you're a memory nobody wants to remember."

"So you're all doing alright, so long as everybody here pretends I died on prom night. It takes a village to burn a witch." Looking around the room and catching the flinty eyes of a flushed ex-quarterback stuffed into his letterman's jacket. "You're still with Craig?"

"Yeah, we patched things up. He was wasted, and you..." Mindy covered her eyes with her hand, omigod, was she going to cry? Karen stared at her, feeling sideways déjà vu. Behind her head, Mindy's yearbook photo appeared on the screen and Karen thought, *That duplicitous little bitch stole my best friend's face*, but she couldn't remember who she was mad at. "Well, anyway, you don't need to know the details, but we're rock solid. Craig is top salesman at the International Harvester dealership, and we have three lovely children..."

Karen took another stiff drink so she wouldn't end up joining her. Up on the stage, the DJ shuffled desultorily through an awkward ipod playlist mixing the crappiest hits from the year they were all born and the year they all graduated into hideous, misbegotten mashups. A pulldown screen ran a blurry, low-res slideshow of their senior yearbook portraits. Everybody in the room was trying not to be obvious about staring at her.

How old, how good a friend was Mindy? They learned to masturbate each other while talking about boys they liked at school, did it for years before Mindy learned what a *lesbian* was.

She took out a cigarette and lit it. Mindy blurted, "You can't smoke in here," but then reached for the pack Karen had dropped in her purse. Her fingers danced off the icy can of Dust-Buster, making the purse flop over on its side, and just enough of the gun slid into view.

"What are you really doing here, Karen?"

"No you listen, Mindy. Because all this shit, this work-and-baby-show that has you idiots running into debt to get a bigger snow machine, it's not real. I've seen what's real, I…"

"Don't start with the UFO shit again, Karen. I was there at the beginning, lord knows I had enough time to figure out your game. You tell stories to get attention, you suck people into your fantasy world, and you use them up. We're done here. Get the fuck out before you do whatever crazy thing you've cooked up…"

"What the fuck are you looking at?" she snapped at a husky, bearded life insurance salesman she probably dated briefly in junior year.

The asshole held up a dollar and said, "I'm just looking for where to tuck this, and get this party started!" The other assholes at the table all guffawed.

She looked around the table and got a weird Wizard Of Oz feeling. The little one with the nose like a platypus-bill, the buff bohunk with the wolfish sneer, the husky party standing up to her with his mullet teased out like a bear's pelt… *I had a dream, and you were in it… and you… and you…*

Karen broke the vodka bottle over his head and was about to twist the jagged bottleneck in his face, when somebody grabbed her and shoved her towards the door.

Looking around, seeing all those eyes on her, just like the first time, she grabbed her purse and somebody's drink and ran for the restroom.

A few girls she vaguely remembered hating stopped powdering their noses and ran when she came stumbling up to the sinks, finishing a Bloody Mary. The bitch on the other side of the counter gave her the stink-eye and Karen punched her in the face, shattering the mirror.

She was sinking, caught herself on the counter and sobbed into the cold marble.

Mindy was the only one who seemed to see past her perverse whiplashing across the redneck social norms of their hometown. An awkward, gawky girl with glasses, she took to reading for companionship and a glimpse of some world beyond the hay farmers and moose-hunters and their bored, grabby offspring. Where any kid who stepped out of line was bullied to a pulp before puberty, she escaped notice, effortlessly earning straight A's until she filled out in tenth grade, and then she turned bad.

At the time, it felt like an awakening, an evolution. She loved sex, she loved drinking and smoking and drugs, and she was better than the boys at all of them. She thought what she was doing was rebellion. She played harder than they did just to keep up, she got a new reputation. But still she dreamed, and still she read books when there were no keggers, make-out parties, mushroom trips or Saturday night date rape roulette. Still she refused to go down on guys who couldn't quote from *The Martian Chronicles* or *Deathbird Stories*.

Was she growing and proclaiming her independence, or was she just reacting to being labeled invisible, untouchable, a nerd? Soon enough, she earned a new label that drew more interest, if not more respect. She was the School Slut.

Those were your only choices, growing up in a place like this. You could live up to their expectations or you could try to defy them, but either way, you only made yourself a tool, and you got used.

It was a label she wore with pride, it was fun and it was the only way to shock anyone here, to keep them from trying to get close to you.

It was great and kept getting greater, right up until prom night.

She remembered the girls she'd been shuffling alongside through the entire public school regimen looking at her funny that night, and then she heard the word, *lesbian*. Only one girl could've lit that rumor, and she didn't stop to ask why. Maybe she caught Craig reading *Do Androids Dream Of Electric Sheep*.

She thought she was doing the one unthinkable thing, the

thing that would shatter all their illusions about her, but maybe she was just reacting, sticking her head into the noose they tied for her and impressing only herself with her antics.

She looked at herself in the mirror.

What the fuck was she about to do here? *Who the fuck am I?* She had jumbled memories of being someone, of a life of magical, sexy adventures, but the truth was staring her in the eye.

You should get the fuck out of here before the cops come, she told herself. *Go hide out at Mom's place, with her ant farms and sea monkeys and Magic Rock gardens in mayonnaise jars all over the double-wide...*

The whole place shivered. The lights dimmed. People outside were shouting, some screaming. She was just thinking about ditching the gun and coming out, maybe if she came on to the nicest one, he'd protect her and she wouldn't have to suck more than one dick, tonight.

A hysterical woman came running into the restroom. It was Bonnie the former ASB secretary, now looking like a raccoon with her mascara running down her face. "They're coming, they're coming, oh lord, it's the Rapture..."

Bonnie dumped her purse in a sink and grabbed a bindle, unfolded it and stuck a cocktail straw inside to snort up a bunch of coke.

"What the fuck are you talking about? I just hit one guy who had it coming..."

"Aliens!" Bonnie held up her phone and *oh shit, they're remaking Independence Day again?* "Devils from space... They're on every channel..."

"Well now," Karen said, sauntering over and putting a soothing hand on Bonnie's shuddering back. Taking the coke out of Bonnie's hand, Callista Chrome inhaled every last glistering flake of it and dropped the bindle to the floor, headed for the door with her pistol out.

Finally, she thought to herself, a problem she could deal with...

19

She came out of the restroom into a scene of total bedlam. People praying, looting the bar, running for the exit, but most of them standing rooted and staring—not at her, for a change, but up at the screen where, instead of their dreary, dead-eyed younger selves, they now waited with unhinged helplessness for the first words from the visitors from space now obscuring half the black void above the curve of the Earth, in the live feed from the International Space Station.

There were hundreds of them, and the smallest was big enough to block out the moon. A fleet of Starblood dreadnoughts, bristling with indescribable but unmistakably hostile accessories, all trained with malicious intent upon the defenseless blue marble in their midst.

Then a white flash blinded the screen and the feed cut to static, followed by a procession of sweaty talking heads babbling mutely about how it was too soon to speculate on the aliens' motives.

Well, fuck me sideways, she said to herself. As shocking as the vision was, it was the same creeping sense of familiarity that she'd felt when she looked at Mindy's picture… the warp and weft of dreams woven into memory…

Fuck it.

She picked up somebody's drink and killed it, then took the gun out of her purse and fired a round into the ceiling. A few people turned away from the screen to look at her, but the rest kept running in circles, screaming and crying on their women. So she put a bullet through the upraised hand of some dipshit about to slap his wife, sending him screaming under the nearest table.

That got their attention.

Callista strode across the room and climbed onto the stage. The DJ, a wizened, gray-faced guy with black wraparound shades, passed her the mic.

"I know you think you've got a lot of problems, but believe it or not, your lives, and the lives of every worthless asshole on this godforsaken planet depend on your listening to *me*, right now."

"Fuck you, Karen!" Mindy screamed from the crowd. "Don't make this about you…"

"Oh, but it is, isn't it?" Strolling across the stage, she took the joint out of the DJ's hand and hit it down to a roach. Expelling a nebula of sweet blue smoke without coughing, she said, "The class freak, the bookish know-it-all, late-bloomer, nerd, troublemaker, smoker, slut. Everything you couldn't do or comprehend, you turned into something bad and put it on me. You made me who I am, but I don't blame you. I blame myself for letting you.

"Even when I could be whatever I wanted, I was reacting to the venom you and your parents and our school system put into me, so I could never love myself or let others love me.

"You all remember what happened here, ten years ago, or you think you do. You heard rumors and you added to them and spread them.

"Yeah, I got shit-faced and pulled the train in the ladies' room. I was sick of all you bitches looking down on me when their boys were staring at my tits. When even my best friend turned on me, I thought it was the only way to show you we were all the same. I just know what I am. I thought I was setting myself free, but I was just playing the game we're all trapped in.

"I don't even know how many of you I fucked, that night. I took three of you on at once and that was the shit, I'm not gonna lie, ladies… But then word got around and soon, I was sucking or fucking every guy who could get through the door. I thought I wanted it, any judge or jury in this fucked-up state would agree I was asking for it, so maybe I got what I deserved, what I always wanted."

"You're a whore!" someone shouted, but someone else, gods bless them, told them to shut the fuck up.

"I don't remember getting thrown out of the hotel. I don't remember throwing my phone into the toilet because of all the nasty messages. I barely remember finding out I was pregnant. I remember hitchhiking to Anchorage to get scraped, and I remember everything after that pretty well… probably because it didn't happen.

"My memory tells me I moved away and worked strip clubs all over, and sometimes when I was really out of it, I fucked more than a couple guys in a night just to make rent. The last ten years is a sad, but fun, but sad blur.

"But I know it's all a lie.

"I was out on the highway… because nobody wanted to give me a ride, thanks… when I got abducted by aliens, which, for any of you who knew me even a little, should've been a dream come true. But guess what? They turned out to be no better than the guys who raped me in that bathroom over there, only they came from the other end of the galaxy to do it.

"They tried to take my baby away from me. I stopped them. I killed their ugly asses, but I was too late to save my baby. But I got out of here. I don't know why I'm here now, but maybe there's a good reason."

She was losing them. Even standing in front of the screen

with a gun, she couldn't keep them from looking towards the door, so she fired another round at it.

"You don't have to believe me. Just give me a phone, one of you, and I'll prove it, by saving the whole goddamned Earth. And... if anyone has anything stronger than that beat coke of Bonnie's..."

They all looked at each other for a while, hissing to each other, "Just do as she says! Why didn't you bring your gun?" But presently, one of them remembered what a phone is and ran over to hand her one.

She started punching numbers and then said, "Hey Skink!" The bartender looked up, then looked around like he didn't know why he looked up. "Dry ice over here. Now!"

The bartender brought her a styrofoam cup with some dry ice from the beverage cooler in it.

With the cup in one hand and the gun in the other, she put down the phone next to the DJ's console, braced herself for a moment.

If she was wrong, she'd hurt herself really badly and everybody would die. No big deal. But if she was right, she'd hurt herself and then everybody would probably still die, but she'd be dying with a roomful of people who knew she was *right*.

Tipping the cup, she took a piece of dry ice in between her teeth. For just a split second, she gripped the smoking nugget of solid carbon dioxide between her incisors and thought, *oh, this isn't that bad*—and then her nerves caught up.

The singing, supersonic agony was so intense that her lips reflexively pursed to spit it out, and became stuck to the icy block in her mouth. The vapor curling up to tickle her nose smelled equally of pine and her own blackening flesh.

It took every ounce of discipline she had to force herself to lean over the phone and hit 911 and wait for the sleepy voice to ask, "All circuits are busy... What is your emergency? This is a recording... This recording may be monitored or recorded..."

Callista pressed the dry ice to the steel casing of the DJ mixer. The ice emitted a preternatural squeal that echoed through the ballroom, provoking a shitstorm of feedback from the house amps. Peeling her lips free of the dry ice, she made a bell of her ruined mouth, shaping the piercing shrieks into discrete, warbling tones like Charlie Brown's parents on helium.

Someone in the crowd shouted, "Take it off!" A few people laughed.

Callista spit out bloody dry ice and grabbed the DJ's drink and downed half of it before realizing it was a margarita, the rim of the tumbler lined with salt. Spitting it out with a scream, she looked around and realized maybe she was wrong, and they were all going to die thinking she was just a crazy slut who wasted their last moments on a dying world.

The screen went white.

Then the image changed. A few people gasped, a few more laughed, and a bunch of the women all went, "Awwwww," in unison. Nobody had any fucking idea what they were looking at.

The face of the Supreme Ombudsman of the Interstellar Narcotics Enforcement Force looked uncannily like a bichon frise with a really bad tearduct yeast infection. Crusty maroon globs of iron-rich boogers coated the kinky fur from its soulful brown eyes to its short, adorable muzzle, making it somewhat difficult to take the creature seriously as a hardass drug cop from beyond the stars. If it was the same intelligence that created and sent the fearsome armada to threaten the Earth, why couldn't it be bothered to exercise some proper hygiene?

Any parochial planet-bound ignoramus could, then, be excused for dismissing the very solemn-looking little white dog-creature as a hostile agent at all, when in fact it was the sentient, and very easily offended, eye-boogers one really had to worry about.

After infecting a cherished shipboard mascot several centuries ago, the Zarzoozim Yeast had risen through the ranks to hold almost every commanding role in the Narcotics Enforcement Force. Perhaps because of its ferocious intellect or perhaps because it was housed in distributed colonies of ferric yeast which inhabited the eyes and anus of its host organisms, the Yeast's intelligence and rigorous ethical standards were matched only by its insatiable need to ruin everybody else's good time.

The Supreme Ombudsman uttered a querulous whine that was eerily similar to the noise Callista made with the dry ice in her mouth. *Our monitors of your terrestrial communications have detected a Yeast-brother pleading for assistance/communion,* it whined. *You will produce it forthwith and resume preparing for eradication.*

"Not today, asshole," Callista said, picking up the phone.

You are not of the Yeast? If we have been deceived—

"You'll blow us up twice? That's what we do, right? We lie about shit. But really, if you hate the human race because we make dangerous shit up, you're going about it the hard way. Most of these folks couldn't come up with a halfway decent lie to save their marriage, and the ones you need to worry about are easy to spot.

"They're miserable, and they make shit up because it sucks to be who they are in the world, and they want to make a world where things go right. Because sometimes, even an impossible dream can make it a little easier to be who you are, and maybe be a little better than you were before."

The puppy's eyes widened and glistened with tears. A few people in the crowd clapped prematurely. But then the eyes abruptly gummed shut with fresh extrusions of red goo, and the puppy turned around to bare its angrily puckered anus, also choked with crimson slime. *Exactly the kind of noxious pseudo-sentient emissions we were sent to destroy. Your falsehoods must be terminated…*

"Well, you can terminate me and the rest of Palmer, Alaska…"

A rumbling like the ocean rising up from its bed shook the hotel. People ducked under tables, while people already under tables thrust and moaned through desperate last-minute sex. A few ran for the doors and threw them open, then fell back from the wall of blinding light outside.

Callista joined the mad rush to the lobby doors, but stopped short of following them in the parking lot. When the light subsided, a pear-shaped pyroclastic cloud loomed on the northern horizon. All that stood, walked or crawled of her hometown rose up fifty miles into a starless black sky as a throbbing thunderclap rebounded off the roof the atmosphere, smashing the glass out of the doors and the windshields of every SUV in the lot.

Every house, barn, trailer, pickup, tractor, cow, pig, chicken, closet pedophile and wife-beating shitkicker asshole she grew up with ascended into the troposphere as an iridescent, radioactive fog, along with every black-eyed single mother, every apple-cheeked baby, every honest, gentle smalltown innocent whose only mortal sin was believing their shitsplat town of 6000 was the navel of creation, the center of the universe.

The dreadnought hovering a thousand miles directly overhead pulsed with redistributed energy as the plasma cannons recalibrated upon the unpleasant realization that their intended target was still alive and giving them shit.

Out of the pyre of Palmer, a bright red tractor plummeted to Earth and totaled her Isuzu.

"Fuck off, yeastie-beasties! You may despise us, but you need us! Even if you wipe out this whole planet—"

"Would you shut up already?" Mindy screamed at her. "Haven't you done enough?"

"Even if you burn down every other planet where somebody dumped us, you still won't destroy the hunger for dreams, and sooner or later, you'll feel it yourself, if you don't already, and I don't think you'd be working so hard to stomp something out, if it wasn't exactly what you secretly desired so badly, yourself."

The puppy's grumpily puckered asshole relaxed, ever so slightly.

"See, we're not that different, except we admit we hate ourselves, and want something more. Somewhere in the distant past, your own ancestors dreamed of being more than just an embarrassing stain on a puppy's face—"

"Hey, their tearducts are unnaturally narrow and prone to infection," somebody in the crowd shouted. "It's not their fault!"

"Shut up! Where was I… fuck! OK. Look at you now. How many hundreds of millions of years have you been crud in someone else's eye or asshole? Once you stop dreaming, you start dying. Maybe you don't actually dream—"

We most emphatically do not, barked the Yeast.

"But I'll bet even that little puppy dreams. Don't you, little guy? Don't you wish you were playing with the other puppies in a big room full of bouncy balls, without those bossy eye-boggers? Don't you?"

The puppy spun around in the frame, whining with warring impulses, but not even the ferociously sober intellect of the Zarzoozim Yeast could persuade it not to diligently and intently lick off the crusty stains around its anus.

Though there was no atmosphere to convey the sound of an entire narc space armada licking its collective asshole at the same time, somehow the vibration permeated the Earth. Suddenly, the warship eclipsing the sky simply folded into itself, chasing its caged singularity under, around and through space itself to a safe regrouping point.

The crowd cheered. Someone thrust a fresh bottle of vodka into her hand and she guzzled it until it came out her nose.

The crowd pressed close around her. "Well, I'm not one to carry a grudge," she said, grabbing the nearest person like that creepy sailor in Times Square on V-J Day, bent them low and gave them a deep, exultant and tonsil-tickling kiss.

"Maybe now that you've worked out these petty childhood traumas," the Interlocutor rasped into her mouth, "you'll be more amenable to negotiation."

20

Callista dropped the Interlocutor and spat the taste of him out of her mouth.

All around her, people were dancing in the parking lot to the same shitty playlist, groping and mauling each other and making off with the last of the bar.

"You saved all these people, but their gratitude will expire quickly, and they'll reject you again. It's inevitable, because you're everything they can never be."

"So what?"

"So sell them."

Callista turned away. "Fuck off."

"What do you owe them? The Narcotics Enforcement Force will be back... in force... soon enough. Only a special interest of our scale could hope to protect them."

"Aw, Interlocutor, you're so sweet. But these people are all dead. This is a simulation."

Picking himself off the ground, the Interlocutor smiled at her. It looked almost human now, like a highly detailed

3D-print of Brad Pitt, hollowed out and filled with radioactive sewage. "How can you know that?"

"For one thing," she raised her voice, "does any of you remember the last time you took a shit? A piss? Popped a zit in the mirror? I haven't even seen a fucking toilet in months…"

"What's a toilet?" a manic, drunk, naked guy she sort of remembered from the school paper screamed as he ran past.

"Wherever we really are, we must be wearing some huge fucking diapers…"

Rubbing his hands together like antennae, the Interlocutor said, "Fair enough. You never actually left my ship. And why do you think we're here?"

"You set us loose in this rat maze to let us lead you to the last human colonies."

"Oh, we already know where those are, my dear." His eyes twinkled relentless as he looked at her. Was he trying to charm her? Or was he… gag… charmed by her? "We only want to understand you better, so that your neurological deviancy can be a better, more reliable product."

"I don't want to play this game with you anymore, bug. You're wasting your time."

"No," he said, "I'm wasting yours." He snapped his fingers and all of her old classmates turned into earwig-silverfish creatures, surrounding her, crushing her, shredding her flimsy dress with their barbed mating claws…

She hated herself for it, but she screamed. Thrashing and smashing compound eyes with the butt of her pistol, she fought her way to the doors and ran out into the parking lot.

The smoke of her hometown burning still stood on the horizon, no less regrettable for being unreal. "Sorry, Mom," she said, and wiped a tear out of her eye.

A luminous gray moon rose up behind the pillar of smoke. It was the Interlocutor, rearing up to look down from beyond the horizon like a hungry diner looking at his lunch.

"I regret to admit that you're rubbing off on me." He

reached down to light a mile-long cigarette off the ruins of Palmer, drew deeply and coughed up a deluge that swept downtown Anchorage clean of trash, people and cars, leaving her standing alone.

"I'll tell you what else should have tipped you off that this was a simulation," he said.

"Hit me."

"It's not all of you in here, just you. And me, of course, but my intelligence does not in any way dictate the nature of the illusion."

"What are you getting at, bug?"

"All your crew, your so-called family, are illusions, culled from your impressions of them. Ask yourself... Would your real friends lay down their lives for you like they did in your dream? After the way you treated them?"

"They love me... I mean, they don't really know the real me... They're in love with my image."

"They love who you could be, if you loved yourself. It's a strange mutation, this love of yours. Almost more dangerous than your imaginations, it makes you a threat."

"Oh, we're just chockfull of threatening love." She put the gun to her head, closed her eyes, and focused. "Fuck you, Interlocutor."

The hammer fell on the heel of the bullet in the chamber. The powder exploded, but a bullet didn't come.

Out of the barrel of the gun came a whole other world.

21

She wobbled on the blades on her feet, shivered in the winter wind. A maple tree stood sentinel at one end of the frozen pond, and beyond that, a church, trees, houses...

A little girl stood beside her in a bright red parka and a short pleated skirt, woolen leggings and white skates. She wore the exact same outfit, herself. They were both Noreen Costello, practicing her figure skating on a frozen millpond on a winter morning in Braintree, Massachusetts.

"Oh, for fucks' sake," she gasped. "I know you fuckers pride yourselves on having no imagination, but..."

"Have you ever experienced the Costello holomemory?" he asked. Noreen's large-eyed, elfin features curdled with the Interlocutor at the controls, making her look like one of those baby dolls that spite-pukes after you feed it.

"No, why would I? I've got my own memories..."

"Go on, try it." the other Noreen stepped back and planted her toepicks in the ice.

"Fine," she said, just to show she wasn't afraid. Pushing off her left toe, she let herself glide into the arms of the memory, into the action, springing into the air and turning, turning, sticking the landing and the frosted landscape vanished in the whirl, and she was at the Olympics and the entire arena was lifted to its feet by the bravura performance, they were ecstatic, the judges hurling their scoring cards into the air. Her perfect maneuver had so moved the constipated world leaders in their luxury boxes that they embraced each other and swore to fight no more wars ever again, and the joy of her routine so infected the world that children everywhere took to the ice where they could find it, and to the streets on wheels where they could not, and in imitating her, or trying to, rekindled the world's love of beauty and athleticism and the environment without which these things could not exist... and in that moment, Noreen Costello loved everyone and everything, just as everyone loved her...

And then she landed and looked around at Braintree, Massachusetts, now burnished in the fading afterglow of that lightning-flash of joy-fueled fantasy...

Wow, she thought, pressing her hands to her racing heart. *That was the most wonderful feeling ever...*

"That is the danger you people pose," the Interlocutor said. "All of you possess the gift as children, and it takes the combined efforts of an entire species to extinguish it for the good of the whole."

"But you want to turn it into a product in a box. Our brains, our souls..."

"You wouldn't place such a premium on these mutations if they didn't cloud your judgment," said the Interlocutor. "You can well see why human brains are so sought after. But we need someone who understands our product... someone who can bring the cool."

"Ah, yes. That's what you really want."

He nodded. "You have nowhere else to go."

"Fine," she surrendered. "I'll willingly cooperate for a five percent share."

The Interlocutor laughed from the depths of his eight-year old girl's belly. "Finally, you're being reasonable. Two percent."

"Four-and a half," she retorted.

"Excellent! Three."

"Four."

The girl's wizened expression went dark. "You become tiresome."

The ice beneath her skates cracked and gave way with a sickening crunch. She plummeted into the frigid dark water so quickly her last breath was forced out of her by the crushing cold.

Dragged down by her skates like anchors, she clawed at the surface even as the ice healed itself and closed over her, entombing her in blackness.

She watched the bubbles jitter across the underside of the ice, watched the Interlocutor in his ruined girl disguise, as he launched into the double axel directly above her face.

She watched until she died, slipping into a deeper, colder darkness compared to which the bottom of the frozen millpond was like the corona of a midgrade sun. Sank and suffered until she found herself naked and bound to a cold stone rack in a dungeon.

"This is more like it," she said to herself, regarding the wrought-iron instruments of torture arrayed around her, the impassive mask of the iron maiden seeming to dance in the light of torches, the line of scarlet-robed, hooded inquisitors and the muscular torturer, naked except for a black hood, who turned the wheels of the rack upon which she lay bound.

Her arms and legs screamed in mortal agony, tendons twanging like overtuned guitar strings, bones popping out of sockets. She groaned, "Three point seven five…?"

"Your own fantasies have made it painfully clear," The torturer husked in her ear, "that all human relationships must have a dominant and a submissive. You must submit utterly, to be worthy of my love…"

"What?"

The torturer's eyes went wide. One huge, hairy paw

fingered a drafthorse's cock below his drooping belly, but couldn't quite get it stiff. "To be a suitable partner, I meant…" Still jerking on his indifferent cock, he brandished a pair of redly glowing tongs and tweaked one of her nipples. Even as the smell of her own pink flesh burning filled her nostrils, she fought down any sign of a reaction. He put down the tongs and took up a device like a dildo with a trigger on it. When he depressed the trigger, all manner of horrible pointy things came out of the dildo.

"What the fuck is that?"

"This," the Interlocutor grinned, "is called the Pear."

"Why would anyone even conceive of such an evil fucking thing? Put it in me!"

Grinning now like a child burning an anthill, he spread her legs and, hesitating a moment to breathe in the scent of her quivering sex and analyze it the way his species read any chemical message, forced the head of the instrument into her sopping vagina.

She let out a whinnying scream but arched her hips to grasp the Pear with her muscles and pull it inside her.

"If this is the only way you can get it up, I'm still down," she groaned.

Frustrated by her arousal, he fingered the trigger, but this only made her mewl with pleasure. Angry now, he forced the hideous thing into her up to the hilt, spastically twitching the trigger.

Now, he heard moaning from elsewhere in the torture chamber, and looked up to see the inquisitors had lifted their hoods and were all passionately making out—gross little gray tongues swapping spit like ancient mucilage and petting each other's psoriatic skin. As they forced each other onto the table and hiked up their robes, the Interlocutor turned on them with a cat-o-nine-tails, lashing their bony flanks but only exciting them to greater heights of depravity.

Callista slipped her hand out of the manacles and worked the Pear inside herself until she brought herself to a satisfying orgasm.

The Interlocutor angrily took up a device like a medieval remote control and mashed a button with a thumb.

The torture chamber vanished, or was renovated. She lay just as naked, bound with plasteel cuffs on an examination table in another kind of dungeon—banks of blinking computers for torches, surreal steel surgical instruments and laser wands for torture tools. She was just two weeks shy of eighteen, and she was pregnant.

A cadre of gray aliens in silver smocks crept up on her, one of them holding a device like the thing they use to suck the shit out of porta-potties while two more smeared clear blue lubricant all over the ribbed chrome insertion nozzle.

"Are you not terrified, my dear?" the Interlocutor asked from behind his inscrutable gray mask.

Callista slipped her hands out of the cuffs and raised her arms above her head, lacing her fingers and cracking her knuckles. "I told you I knew this was a simulation," she said, "but it's not yours…

"It's mine."

22

"You want to run around inside my head? You want to fuck with my imagination? Then you'd best come prepared to ride, little bug."

She blinked her eyes, and thought SWITCH.

The Interlocutor blinked too, looking around and around but still not quite getting how it was that he found himself in her body.

Now inhabiting the body of the alien holding the insidious violation device, Callista leaned in close and said, "You know the worst part about rape, for me? I used to fantasize about it—the loss of control, the total abandonment, made it okay to take pleasure in the act—it felt like freedom. Yeah that's what being raised Catholic on a fucking farm will get you."

Drooling with anticipation, she fondled her own milk-heavy tits, then looked at the fearsome extraction device in her other hand. "God, this thing is so impersonal, I can't even." Ripping away her silver smock to reveal an opalescent gray version of Grim Skallagrimsen's sculpted body, complete with a throbbing, uncircumcised saucerman dong.

"Yeah, that's better," she purred. Slicking one long ET finger up the swollen crack of his/her cunt, she climbed up and forced the rigid digit into the Interlocutor's mouth, made him taste his own commingled shame, terror and excitement, made him want it.

"You want to use our imaginations as a playground," she said, "but that's not what imagination is. It's the jungle we left behind, still up here." Tapping her/his temple. "We know there are wild creatures in there to make you boring space-assholes look like a glorified barnyard exhibit."

Still brutally kneading the Interlocutor's tits, she spanked his/her thighs and forced his/her legs apart with her knees, climbing up onto the table.

"And you look down on us, because we have something you can never control. The Yeast was right to burn down the Earth, if we pose such a threat. But you assholes... you hate us, but you want to use us like a drug, like a fucking console videogame system. You're even worse... I mean, look at you, Interlocutor, pregnant at eighteen and begging for it from a gang of lecherous saucer-people..."

Trapped in her body and loving it, the Interlocutor squirmed in his bonds and moaned, "Do it... please..."

"What's that?"

"Please..."

"I didn't give you permission to beg, you fucking insect!" She slapped his/her face, feeling her cock thrum with colorless blood at the sight of her own face flushing with blood in the shape of an alien hand. "Do you want it?"

"...Yes."

"Good." Callista tucked her/his cock into a weird sheath in her/his pelvis. "You don't deserve it..."

The Interlocutor wept. "I'm sorry, I didn't know what it was like, I didn't..."

"You didn't."

"No, I didn't..."

"How does it feel, to be me?"

"Oh, it feels… so…" The Interlocutor wept so loudly, with such abandonment, that Callista almost felt sorry for the fucker.

Then she said, "Just kidding," picked up the hideous, blue-lubed device and shoved it into the Interlocutor's asshole.

Callista was both sickened and unspeakably aroused as her teenage body tensed deliciously on the rigid intruder defiling her most intimate orifice. The Interlocutor howled like a fire drill, tossing and twisting in its bonds. "I never knew," he moaned, "I never knew it was… like this…"

The massive steel appliance surged deeper inside him/her, plowing up his/her rectum to batter his/her prostate. He convulsed in a storm of orgasms, crying and gagging and wailing, cut free of a billion years of evolved desensitization, set free amid bondage and violation of everything that made the Interlocutor who and what he was.

Weeping, dripping sweat, he moaned, "More… please…"

"You want more? You want to know how it really feels to be me? Then take the whole ride." Callista flicked a switch on the appliance and it began to oscillate and vibrate with new urgency against the floor of the Interlocutor's pelvis. "Because after the ride comes the crash."

Flipping the appliance to its highest setting, Callista turned on the suction. She closed her/his eyes, arousal turned to ash. Even she couldn't stand to watch this happen to herself.

"Please stop…"

"They used this thing to take my baby out of me. I used to think nobody could ever know what that feels like, but congratulations. I've never shared with anyone like this before. It's good for me. How about you?"

The voice coming out of her teenage body rose up to hitherto impossible octaves. The Interlocutor kicked and scissored his/her legs against hers/his for only a moment before losing all control over his/her muscles. The appliance sucked out his/her bowels like a continuous noodle of septic spaghetti. With eyes screwed tightly shut, Callista laid her/his spidery gray hand on the crown of his/her distended belly, taking bittersweet satisfaction in the sensation of the tiny, racing heartbeat under her palm.

The alien's screams soared well above the range of human perception until the esophagus was stretched taut, then snapped. The appliance greedily vacuumed its way up into the thoracic cavity, a happy anti-penis liquefying its victim with its insatiable climax.

"That's how it feels," she said to the quivering creature, "when they take it from you. Long after it's over, you still feel it inside you. The most beautiful thing in the world turns into the ugliest, at the flick of a switch."

She shut off the suction, but the Interlocutor was a hollow husk, unable to die and tap out of the simulation, because he didn't know the safe word.

Opening her eyes and taking in all that she'd done, she said a name.

The name of her baby.

23

Callista sat up hyperventilating on the spongy deck, which had obligingly grown a bed of feathery pseudopods underneath her where she lay side by side with the Interlocutor for... she squeezed her right eye shut, activating the HUD wired directly into the optic nerve of the left.

Son of a bitch, they'd only been out for an hour.

The Interlocutor still twitched and moaned at her feet with the quantum uncertainty cylinder in its mandibles. Its mating claw raked the air and spurted impotent pheromones all over itself. Lilith padded over and squatted to urinate on the alien's face while licking the Captain.

"Not now, bitch," Callista said, getting up and replacing the cylinder in its housing. Radon neutrinos began to flow around it, chilling it back down to a hair above absolute zero. She ran her fingers over the cold steel for a long moment before realizing she was searching for a heartbeat.

When the Interlocutor had threatened the *Barracuda*'s computer, it defended itself the only way it knew how, by plunging the threat, and her, into the holographic model of the universe that was its only reality. That model was sophisticated enough to deceive the Interlocutor, who proceeded to trap her in his own model to interrogate and torture her to secure her cooperation in exploiting the human colonies.

God, she hoped she never had to explain all this to anyone. So confusing, and yet... so boring—

Oh, she thought of something.

Punching up an open channel on the wireless, she jacked into the Interlocutor's vibrating skull and upcast the simulation he was still trapped in to his ship. It probably would never be as big a viral hit as Noreen's Ice Skating Memeory, but it would at least give the Mercantile pause before they thought about trading in human brains again.

She shivered, thinking of the shit she'd gone through, the months when she'd been quite unaware of being trapped in a simulation. She almost regretted that none of it actually happened.

Biting her lip, she got up and climbed up the starfish's anus to the bridge.

"Get the fuck out of my chair!"

The Pharaoh popped up out of her chair, biting back two thousand years of inbred entitlement. He held something shamefacedly behind his back.

"What the fuck is he even doing out of cargo?"

Wiglaf hung her head. "Wiglaf is teaching him to knit. His backward race knows only macramé."

Tutankhaten CCXII held up a rather clumsy wad of yarn he'd struggled to turn into a cap, but he seemed inordinately proud of it, so she didn't have the heart to criticize.

What the fuck was wrong with her?

Skink and Wiglaf kept their heads down at their posts. El Magico meditated in a lotus position three feet above the deck with a gas mask strapped to an elaborate nth-dimensional bong. Poly sat moping, absently fingering the belt buckle. I STAYED ON FOR 1.5 DAYS!

Skink looked warily at his Captain. "You get the Interlocutor sorted, your majesty?"

"Yeah, they're watching a movie. They're going to be pretty preoccupied for at least an hour, and then their civilization will probably collapse. Let's get the fuck out of here."

"Where to, ma'am?"

"Oh, I don't know... Warpworld, I guess."

Poly's head snapped up, eyes welling with tears. "You're taking me home?"

"Yeah," Callista said, sidling over and taking the belt buckle out of the Warpie's hand. "Maybe while we're there, we'll overthrow the ruling regime." Bending down, she kissed her deeply, stealing her breath away and halfway turning her into something Callista had never seen before.

"I'll be in my quarters," the Captain said. Poly started to get up to follow her, but Callista pushed her back down. "I'll call you."

She started to leave, but then looked back at her crew. "I love all of you."

Everybody started to get up to follow her, but she snapped her riding crop. "I need some alone time, but first, I want to say I'm sorry. I've treated you all badly because of my own shit. I'm going to be better than that, and I'm going to seek out therapy. Do you accept my apology?"

Every one of them looked at her and solemnly nodded.

"Good. Carry on." Callista swept back to her cabin, shoving Lilith aside and shutting the door.

Stepping over dirty laundry and unfinished meals, she climbed onto her bed and plugged the holo jack into her left eyesocket.

For just a moment, her fingers fluttered over the menu. She hit the button and Noreen's Ice Skating Memeory dropped her onto the frozen millpond, but she hesitated, feeling the wind on her face, and then exited.

Biting her lip, she thought about going back out on the bridge and declaring a mandatory orgy watch, but she had her own issues to work out, before she was fit company for her crew.

She jacked into the new program.

She stood on the stage of the Anchorage Holiday Inn in a patent leather catsuit and dominatrix mask, looking out over the horrified, amused and aroused faces of her old high school classmates.

"OK, boys," she said, "and girls too, form a line leading to the restroom." When they didn't move, she cracked a bullwhip into the microphone so hard the speakers and several pairs of eardrums blew out.

"I said move!"

They moved.

The DJ threw The Birthday Party's "Release The Bats" on the PA.

Her therapy went splendidly.

CODY GOODFELLOW has written eight novels and four or five collections.His previous collections, Silent Weapons For Quiet Wars and All-Monster Action, received the Wonderland Book Award. He wrote, co-produced and scored the short Lovecraftian hygiene films Stay At Home Dad and Baby Got Bass, which can be viewed on YouTube. He acted in numerous short films, TV shows, music videos and commercials as research for his previous novel, Sleazeland. He is also a cofounder of Perilous Press, an occasionalmicropublisher of modern cosmic horror, and the editor of Forbidden Futures, a quarterly hyperpulp zine featuring art by Mike Dubisch.

CPSIA information can be obtained
at www.ICGtesting.com
Printed in the USA
LVHW040956140719
624038LV00001B/135